Black Beauty Presents BRINGS YOU

Alexis & Wesley: Addicted to a Street King

WRITTEN BY R. COXTON &

DEIDRE LESHAY

ACKNOWLEGEMENTS

Randy and Deidre would like to thank God, without him none of this would even be possible. Next, we would like to say thank you to all of the readers. You guys are the best and we thank you from the bottom of our hearts.

Contents

ALEXIS

I sat on the edge of the hotel bed, freaking the fuck out as I looked down at Wesley Mayfield's lifeless body. He had been my kryptonite cheating partner, my lover, and my friend.

I'm Alexis Goodwin Manchester, married, news reporter, social interest leader, and cheating wife. That wouldn't sound good on breaking news. Damn, I thought, trying to get my thoughts together.

I was meeting Wesley for my weekly dose of 'get right.' I said I was married but something about that black dick I couldn't shake. My husband was Chase Manchester, the chief of police, a good all-American, blonde-haired, blue-eyed boy. He was my rebound from a bad relationship. Chase knew that my heart was jaded to love in the beginning. Wesley and I had dealt with each other casually in the past; I never hid that from Chase. That's why anytime he could rouse or piss Wesley off, he would do so with his authority.

Don't get me wrong, Chase was a good husband and provider, but he had major shortcomings in the bedroom. Let's just be frank, my husband had a small dick and he barely scratched the surface. He wasn't sexually aggressive in the bedroom. He always wanted to give it to me slow and sexy, but sometimes a girl just needed a man to throw her on the bed and fuck the life out of her and then fuck the life back in her. I wouldn't make any excuses for my cheating, however this was how I got here. I needed something sexually that my husband couldn't offer me.

I should've had more self-control and been able to walk away from my past, but now I needed to figure out how I could disassociate myself from this. I was sure someone saw me walking in here. I was used to reporting the news, not being part of it and Wesley being the street king he was, guaranteed front-page coverage.

Alexis & Wesley: Addicted to a Street King   R. Coxton

Now, how the fuck would I get him out of here? I was way too cute for jail. *Damn it, think, Alexis, think.* All black girls looked like me so the first thing I needed to do was change my hairstyle. Then I turned my cell phone off. I was on the other side of town the last time I made a call so there was no way that I was being tracked on any towers. Thank God I got rid of that On-Star. There was really no way for anyone to know that I was here.

Oh yeah, my fingerprints were all over the place. There were cleaning supplies in my car. I had been to the Dollar Tree earlier this week and I was too lazy to take the shit in the house, not to mention that I had my car cleaning kit in my trunk as well. I put on my shades and held my head down as I ran to my car, grabbed my utility tote, and went back in the room. I sprayed bleach on everything I thought that I had touched, then removed the sheets from the bed, placing them in my tote. I didn't need my hair left anywhere. I had a mini vacuum in that tote so I used it to vacuum the bed and the pillows. Then around his body, a part of me wanted to cry. I loved this man and I didn't mean to kill him. I was in love with him, but I couldn't have him telling Chase about our affair and I couldn't allow him to stop me from getting this abortion. I had no idea how I would explain this black eye. I took a towel from my utility tote and took the knife out of him. I decided that I would have to set his ass on fire to get rid of any DNA that I might have left on him.

CHASE

I'd been calling Alexis for hours; usually we would talk during the day. But both of us had demanding jobs. I was rise and shine every morning at four a.m.; my morning was packed with meetings. Alexis, with her job as a news reporter, had a little more flexibility so a lot of the household responsibilities fell on her.

My thoughts went back to the first time I met her. It was a double homicide. I saw her at the crime scene. I was a lieutenant then. I was in love at first sight. I loved her persistence. She wore a black fitted skirt, with a white silk blouse. Her ebony eyes were like pools and I was ready to dive into them; her hair was styled in a bob cut.

We had our first run-in when she interviewed me about the case, but I could tell she was career driven, motivated by a broken heart. She was inviting but distant. I learned quickly it would take a lot to sway her. After our initial meeting, I decided to do my homework. I saw she had ties to my nemesis Wesley Mayfield. He ran the Gucci Cartel. I couldn't link the two together, but after digging deeper, I realized they had a connection, a past, before she even told me. I was never one to date outside my race, but something about Alexis—I had to have her as mine. The fact that she was a public figure would get her past the sneers and jeers of my family and friends.

I envisioned us as a power couple. Was I lusting after this mocha goddess? Yes, I was but I considered being persistent. I was her future; she just didn't know it in the beginning. She just viewed me as another white guy who wasn't her flavor. I have to admit I did go to extremes to make her mine. I knew she was addicted to Wesley. He didn't deserve her. I turned up the harassment on him once I knew he was my competition. Alexis and I crossed paths more with the murder rate increasing in the city. After months of asking her to dinner, she finally gave in. All the while, I had my guys keeping Wesley preoccupied so I could accomplish making her mine.

My phone rang, bringing me back to reality. I assumed that it was Alexis. Imagine my disappointment when it was a call reporting a homicide at the Hilton. I rose from my desk, stopping at my friend Elliott's desk to ask him to send a car by my house. Not hearing from Alexis had me worried out of my mind. He agreed that he would call me and let me know that she was all right. As I headed to my car, I called Alexis' job to see if she was working on a story. It wasn't like her to go the whole day without talking to me. I prayed that she was okay. Fifteen minutes later, I was at the Hilton. I went to Room 4631. It reeked of burning flesh. One of the officers on the scene said that it was Wesley Mayfield. He had really pissed someone off. The M.E. Sasha Hicks said that she needed to examine the body before she could confirm the true cause of death. *Damn, how will I break the news to Alexis?*

Shit was about to get real. The streets would definitely seek revenge and with cuts I had just faced, my force couldn't handle.

Nine months earlier….

ALEXIS

I walked into the Vogue Lounge as usual. Wesley had a flock of chicks cheesing in his face. I knew he saw me but he had to be the center of attention. I just smiled and made my way to my table.

When we were younger, attention was something that he lacked. Both of his parents were addicts. He didn't have the latest gear, or a lot of friends in school, but those factors fueled his drive.

I always watched him from afar. He was always hustling to support himself. He was an only child but his parents had custody of his cousin Carlton. Eventually, Wesley and his cousin were adopted by a Russian mafia head named Afon. Afon loved Wesley and Carlton's hustler spirit so he provided them with the essentials to achieve the attention he longed for.

Sorry I got sidetracked. Vogue Lounge was owned by Afon and the Gucci Cartel. It was full to the max tonight with hustlers, thirst buckets, and wannabe hittas. Wesley and I had an unspoken situation. He was every woman's perfect guy; even though he was hood, he was multi-diverse.

The first time we hung out we went rock climbing. Our second date we went Salsa dancing. I knew he wasn't good for me, but I enjoyed what he offered.

Before going to the table, I stopped at the bar for a drink. Chase was meeting me here, but it would be about twenty minutes before he got here. As I ordered my drink, Wesley slipped up beside me, flashing his beautiful smile.

"So, is that pussy mine for tonight?" he whispered in my ear.

I smiled as my kitty purred at his comment.

"You seem to already have your hands full," I flirted back. "You're looking dapper tonight." I lusted over him in a black Gucci suit with a matching black shirt and tie. His dreads were braided back, causing his two-carat earring to almost blind me.

"You're looking quite tasty as well," he chimed.

I took in the scowls, side-eyes as we exchanged pleasantries from damn near every woman in the room.

"You know how we get down. I know your situation, you know mine," Wesley assured me.

"Well, go back and entertain your groupies. You know my number," I smiled.

"Most definitely, Alexis." He smiled as he made his way back to his table. Before he left, he made sure to pay for my drink.

He thought he was so smooth with his sexy ass.

WESLEY

That damn Alexis knew she belonged to me, not that square-ass cop Chase. I sat back as I looked at all the women that flooded my club. I could have each one hands down. I wanted the one that was getting married. Ain't that about a bitch, I sighed to myself. I could admit I fucked it up, chasing after worthless bitches who brought nothing to the table other than pussy, and some fiyah ass head. I was constantly disrespecting her with unworthy-ass women. Her favorite response to shield the pain was, "We just fucking; you're not my nigga."

I knew she was in love with me regardless of what I did. She gave me a pass, so I thought. But what I didn't know was that she had her own shit brewing that rocked my world. I remembered that shit like it was yesterday. I was chilling in the Excelsior with my crew like I always did, popping bottles, talking shit like we do. Bitches surrounded us like we owned the club. I had talked to Alexis earlier. She told me she was chilling. I was fucked up when I saw her ass walk in hand in hand with Chase, white preppy-dressed ass. She looked good as hell, dressed in a blue maxi dress that hugged her curves. This muthafucka was flossing what was mine. My crew didn't help it by making sure I acknowledged their asses. I rose up from my table, with my 9mm tucked in my waist under my jacket. I knew I was wrong. I had done my shit to her but for her to showcase this cracker in my face in public had my black ass heated.

I rolled up to her table then barked, "Let me holla at you for a minute." Chase and I locked eyes. I wanted him to say something. I would've emptied my clip into his ass.

"Wesley, now isn't a good time. I'll call you later," she responded, flashing her pearly whites. I was shocked. Honestly, I expected her ass to jump to bark. Chase stared at me and I almost made a scene, but I'll be damned if I let her ass know she hurt my feelings showing up with this fool.

"All right, Alexis. I guess I'll get up with you later." I responded as I walked away.

The first muthafucka to make a smart-ass remark was getting one in the head, I thought as I walked away.

***

I walked around Concord Mills with some meaningless bitch and I saw her in Camella La Vie, a fucking dress store. Her ass was trying on wedding dresses. I did what any man would do in my situation. I told my groupie to have a seat while I put Alexis' ass in check. I waltzed my ass in that store and screamed her name. She turned, looking at me with tears in her eyes. She walked over to me.

"I've been calling you for three fucking months. You can't call a nigga back."

"Hey, Wesley, it's good to see you too. I've been great, thank you for not asking. How are you? Still running around with silly bitches, I see."

"Why haven't you been taking my calls?" I asked her again.

"Because you were looking for bitches to fuck and I'm the woman that you should want to marry. I won't be anyone's main choice. I want to be a man's only choice, and I get that with Chase. So, he asked me to marry him and I accepted. He loves me."

"WHAT THE FUCK, ALEXIS? I LOVE YOU." I yelled at her.

We stood there looking at each other and before I knew it, I grabbed her, kissing her. She needed to know that I wanted her. She broke our kiss.

"Look, Wesley, I'm about to get married; it's too late."

"Please just have dinner with me." I pleaded and she knew I wasn't the nigga to beg.

"Fine, you have to cook me dinner. I can't risk any of Chase's friends seeing us together."

Alexis & Wesley: Addicted to a Street King   Deidre Leshay

"Fine, come over at seven p.m. sharp."

She agreed. As she walked away, I bet her ass was smiling. She would give me that pussy tonight. I thought as I walked out of the store. Alexis got my ass all in my feeling, wanting to kill her and that square-ass cracker. I looked at my watch. It was four now, so I pulled out my phone to cancel plans I had for tonight. Thirty minutes later, I was at the house, cooking for her ass like I was some little bitch. I pulled out some Porterhouse steaks I planned to smother with mushrooms and onions, with some rice pilaf. I also warmed up some Hawaiian rolls. An hour later, I plated the food minutes before seven p.m. A nigga anxious because I knew I had to mark this pussy again to get her mind right back on my team.

I called her, "Where are you?"

"I'm coming up on the elevator now," she sighed. I made sure I was on point as I wore a grey Jordan jogger suit with the newest Kevin Durant's. I knew this Gucci Red cologne would have that pussy wetter than a river. Minutes later, she entered my spot. Alexis looked good as hell wearing some Levi jeans with a red tee, and stilettos showing her freshly painted toes. I had to admit she had a muthafucka fucked up. I was definitely kicking myself in the ass. Hindsight was twenty-twenty.

"So, am I on the do-not-call list?" I questioned as she sat down at the table.

"Why are you tripping? We were just fucking. I moved on," she responded.

That fact she was taking this lightly pissed me off, but I played it cool.

"So, you think this shit a joke?" I grumbled.

She just smiled. I yanked her ass up, pressing her against my bar.

"Let me the fuck go," she snapped. "Do you not know who the fuck my fiancé is?" she continued.

I unfastened her pants as I applied all my weight against her.

"I don't give a fuck who he is," I boasted as I shoved my tongue into her mouth as my fingers made their way down to her sloppy, wet pussy.

"Ooh shit," she gasped as she started sucking my tongue.

I forcibly pulled her jeans around her ankles as I spun her around. Her ass poked out as I pulled my jogging pants down. My hard dick almost ripped through my boxers. She reached back to stroke it as I kissed her neck. I whispered in her ear as I drove my dick into her, "You missed this dick, didn't you?" I said as I plunged my dick into her waiting wet pussy.

She moaned aloud, "Fuck, I missed this good-ass dick."

I smiled to myself. I worked this dick in her pussy like a madman. I had her pinned against the wall as her pussy juices soaked my dick. Typically, she would throw it back but she was taking it. Her ass was so stubborn; she enjoyed the dick but tried to fight the pleasure at the same time. She took this dick today. I started to suck on her neck and she let out a moan. I must not be deep enough so I pulled her left up, changing my motion. She arched her back and moved her hips. We were back to the groove. To add more pleasure, I grabbed a handful of her hair.

"This is my pussy."

"Yes, Daddy, this is your pussy," she agreed. "Yes, it's yours," she said breathlessly.

I bet her ass wouldn't be marrying that whack-ass white boy now.

CHASE

I walked in the house at midnight thinking I'd be greeted by my beautiful fiancé, but she wasn't there and her phone went straight to voicemail. She must be working late as I headed to the shower. I washed, got out, and she still wasn't there. I checked the microwave and found a plate with a note.

Chase,

I'm going to hang out with an old friend. Don't wait up.

I love you,

Alexis

I warmed up my food and went to bed. Four a.m. came early. I lay there watching the clock. It was after three thirty a.m. when Alexis stumbled in the house, walking like she had hurt herself. She smelled like she had just gotten out of the shower. I knew she had been with Wesley in the back of my mind. *How could she betray me?* I thought to myself as she undressed, thinking I was sleeping. What she didn't know was her disrespect to me made Wesley and his crew enemy number one. I had invested too much time into her to let Wesley or anyone else fuck up what we had. I had let him live and get rich in my city long enough. I had my guys trailing Wesley for months now. After their tryst tonight, they would hate me with a passion, but I had to show them who was really running shit. As I dressed for work, I watched as she slept peacefully, pissed to the max that she would be so bold as to fuck Wesley, and then come lay in my bed like it was all good. The more I looked at her, the madder I fucking got, knowing she had been with him, fucking him after she told me she was done with him. As I walked in the kitchen for my morning coffee, I thought to myself, if I let her get away with this shit, she would keep trying to treat me with disrespect. I grabbed a bowl, filled it with water and ice. As I stormed in the room, I stopped for a minute. She looked so fucking beautiful. I walked closer to the bed, and dumped it on her.

"What the fuck?" escaped her lips as she abruptly awoke.

I smiled then questioned her, "You just can't leave his ass alone, can you?"

Shivering, still soaked and pissed, she sat up and lied, "Who, what the hell you talking about, Chase?"

The fact that she was willing to lie only added fuel to the fire. I moved closer as I sat on the dry side of the bed. She rose from the bed to get dressed.

"So, you're really gonna fucking lie to me," I growled.

"Chase, it's too fucking early for your insecurities," she defended.

"I fucking know I smelled the different soap on you," I snapped.

Knowing that I was right, a silence fell between us. It was my sign that she had strayed. I wanted to choke the shit out of her, no lie, but I just grabbed my coffee thermos and left.

ALEXIS

Damn, I thought as I got out the bed, *I cannot believe that I fucked Wesley last night.* What the hell was I thinking going over there? I just wanted to have an innocent dinner with him. The horrible part about all this was the sex was amazing. He always satisfied me, but he left me wanting to come back for more. My goal was to leave his ass alone, but no, I had to play right into his nest. I didn't even make his ass use protection. *Damn it, Alexis, how in the world could you be so damn stupid?* Only God knew how many nasty-ass bitches his ass had been laid up with him. Damn. I really needed to fix things with Chase. I never meant to hurt him and it wasn't my plan to sleep with Wesley.

Just the thought of Wesley made my pussy wet. I wanted to feel him inside me. I wanted to kiss his lips and taste him. Damn it, why couldn't he just do right. That was what I had to keep telling myself. Wesley would never do right by me, so there was no need to waste my time. Chase, on the other hand, was loving and loyal. I had to make this right with him. I decided to send him a text.

"Hey, babe. Look, I'm sorry. It was disrespectful for me to stay out all night, but it wasn't what you think."

"What was it then, Alexis?"

I could tell that he was still pissed; he never called me by my name. I had no idea how to tell him I was out all night fucking. I didn't want to lie to him but I would try to avoid it as much as possible.

"I was out with my friends and I lost track of time. The fresh scent you smelled was lotion; it wasn't a new soap. Babe, I love you more than anything and would never do anything to jeopardize that, babe."

"That sounds like bullshit, Alexis. So, hit me back when you learn how to tell the truth."

"Why are you dead set on me cheating? If you want me to go fuck Wesley, then fine, Chase. I will call him and go fuck him."

"Fuck you, Alexis."

"Who the fuck are you talking to? I'm not one of them sorry-ass white bitches that you're used to fucking. FUCK YOU, CHASE."

In the process of trying to fix things, he just wanted to accuse me of cheating on him when he was unable to prove that shit.

I had to get ready for work so I changed the bed, then found something to wear. As I was leaving the house, as soon as I got in my car, my phone rang. I knew that Chase had got his mind right, but no, it was Wesley. I sent his ass to voicemail. I made it through the whole day and nothing from Chase at all. I just happened to be heading home, I was at the stoplight and saw Chase all hugged up with some bitch. His ass was supposed to be at work. I watched them walk in her house. I made a U-turn in the middle of the street, damn near hitting three cars. I parked right behind his car. Running to her door and beating on it like a mad woman, she opened it. I burst past her, running to Chase, and punched him in the eye.

"NO WONDER YOU ARE ACCUSING ME OF CHEATING. YOU THINK THAT YOU CAN JUST FUCK THE NEXT BITCH? IS THIS WHY YOU ACCUSED ME OF CHEATING?"

Before he could reply, I punched his ass again. Then walked out of the house.

WESLEY

Seven a.m. this morning, I got a call from the county jail. I hesitated to answer.

"Speak," I barked into the phone.

"Cuz, them narcos raided us this morning," he chimed.

"No shit, that fucking Chase. That white boy must have found out I fucked Alexis," I laughed to myself.

"Cuz, that pussy is not worth our money," snapped Carlton.

I wondered why Alexis hadn't called me, especially after I beat them guts up. Carlton was right; we didn't need this type of heat.

"How many did they lock up?" I questioned.

"Including me, three others from our spot on West Boulevard," he responded.

"Okay, let me hop off here and holla at Mackins Bonding about getting y'all out," I assured Carlton.

"Cuzzo, real talk. Let her go; we got too much to lose," said Carlton before we ended the call.

Was Carlton out of his fucking mind? There was no way in hell I would let her go. That white boy was trying to steal my shit and I wouldn't let it go down like that. When this was all over, Alexis would be right next to me.

What Chase didn't know was that the little breezy Camille he was fucking with was a dancer in my strip club, Fantasie's. I needed to keep his chocolate-loving ass distracted. Camille did just the trick. I needed her to turn his ass out and just maybe, he would leave Alexis or it would just give me more time with her. She just needed one more dose of this dick and things would work themselves out.

Alexis' ass had been trying to put me on the backburner; that shit ain't happening. I hadn't talked to her ass in two fucking weeks. I didn't know why she acted as if she didn't get the memo that she was my property.

That white boy was just borrowing her ass until I figured out what I wanted to do to get things back on track with her. I knew I loved her, but she was a public figure. I was on the opposite end of the spectrum, and I didn't want my dealings to affect her career. I would never want my dirt to damage her.

I attempted to call her; there was no answer. I sent some flowers to her job, asking her to call me.

She could make me send the goons after her ass.

ALEXIS

I couldn't believe his hypocrite ass cheated on me. I felt like shit after my episode with Wesley, and this muthafucka had the nerve to call me on my shit while his ass was out here tricking with these thirsty-ass hoes.

I was pissed, but relieved his ass was cheating. I just wanted to knock his fucking head off. I never would've thought that he was a cheater. I put his ass on a pedestal while staying away from Wesley out of respect for him. And this was the fucking thanks I got.

But, what he didn't know, I would still marry his ass; ultimately Chase was the better choice. I just had to show him my crazy girl side. On the other hand, Wesley just got an unlimited pass to this pussy. Wesley had been calling me all morning. He just thought that I would drop everything and run when he called. Let me text his ass.

"It's not a good time, Wes."

In two hours, it needed to be a great fucking time.

I needed Wesley to calm down. Chase wanted a war with Wesley. He didn't want those types of problems. After the shit he pulled a few days ago, he better not say shit about my whereabouts or what I was doing.

Tears streamed down my face as I packed my overnight bag with no destination in mind. I left Wesley for cheating, so there was no way in hell I would let Chase's punk ass put me through the same shit.

Just as I was walking out the door, Chase came in. We glared at each other. I folded my arms. I really didn't want to hear what he had to say, but I knew that it was coming whether I liked it or not. Poor Chase had a black eye, but he still looked extremely sad and hurt.

"Babe, can we sit down and talk?"

"Why, Chase, to accuse me of more bullshit that you are doing and feel guilty about?"

"I'm sorry. A few of my cop buddies said that they had seen you with Wesley in the mall."

"Really, Chase, you let some outsiders sell out your future wife? Yes, I talked to him in the mall. He saw me trying on my wedding dress and he stopped in to say hi and to talk shit to me for not fucking with him. Why didn't you just ask me about it?"

"I let my ego get the best of me. I'm sorry."

Damn, I was just as guilty as his ass, but he couldn't prove it. Now he looked extra stupid. I bet he would work real hard to keep me.

"How long have you been fucking that stripper?"

"Once or twice, but that shit didn't mean anything to me. I was there for Mike's bachelor party and she was all over me. After a lot of drinks, I let the bitch give me head. After that, we hooked up again, then last night, but we didn't fuck."

"You didn't come home last night, so where were you?"

"Okay fine, I fucked her but only because I really thought that you were with Wesley."

I almost hit his ass for lying to me, but I managed to keep it together. There was no need for me to act crazy; the ball was in my court.

"Chase, I need to take some time to process all this. You are no better than Wesley. I left him because I thought that you were different and I thought that you would love and honor me. I won't share the man that I love."

"I don't want you to go. Baby, I'm sorry. Can we please work this out?"

"Right now, I just need time to clear my head. I'm going to the Hilton."

Chase went to say something, but I walked out the door with tears falling down my cheeks.

CHASE

Alexis just left me. What the fuck was I thinking? I thought to myself as I sat at my desk. I never meant for Alexis to find out about Camille. I fucked up. She wasn't shit to me, just a piece of easy stripper ass. She knew I was with Alexis, and played her part. I knew with us being in public it heightened our chances of getting caught. I met her at one of Wesley's clubs. She was the featured dancer. We flirted with each other the whole night and I had to have her after she sucked the life out of me.

Don't get me wrong, Alexis was on point as far as satisfying me on all levels, but she never sucked my dick like that. I was just being a man who saw an easy piece of ass.

She drew me in with her sob story; she said she was only dancing to pay for school but after dealing with her, I later learned that was a lie. Plus, that juicy ass of hers was hypnotic. It was amazing how as I got older, my taste in women changed. Before I hit my late twenties, my flavor was blondes with big tits, a flat ass.

Alexis messed me up. She was like a chocolate goddess and I fell prey so there was no way some broad on a come-up like Camille wasn't about to fuck up what we had, and neither was that street thug Wesley. I knew he told Camille to fuck me and I would make his ass pay for that. Last night was a total setup and my ass fell for it. I wouldn't stop until Alexis was all mine. My desk phone rang.

"So, Carlton and the rest of Wesley's goons got out?" I asked the intake sergeant.

"Yeah, Chief, they were just bonded out by Mackins Bonding."

"Fuck."

"What's wrong, Chief?"

"Nothing," I answered as I ended the call.

Damn, I was hoping that those fuck boys would spend a little time in jail or snitch on Wesley, but it was death before dishonor in the streets. I picked up the phone and dialed Alexis, but she didn't answer. Her ass sent me to voicemail. I left her a message, telling her that I was sorry and I hoped she could find it in her to forgive me.

WESLEY

I smiled as Carlton and my crew walked into the clubhouse.

"Wassup, jailbirds?" I joked as they filed in. I dapped each one up as they came past.

"What's popping, boss?" they all asked in unison.

"Glad to see my squad out of those steel cages." Carlton gave me a non-approving look like he was ready to blurt something out. I looked at him and said, "Speak on it, cuz, before you burst."

By the fact that he didn't blurt what he had to say, he was searching for the right words.

"We don't n eed those crackers blowing us up over you dipping into his woman's pussy," growled Carlton.

I knew he was speaking the truth, but I was addicted to Alexis and wasn't trying to hear it, seeing I was just in them guts last night.

"Man, I know but I'm Pookie when it comes to her," I joked but I could see the seriousness in his face.

I took a toke off my blunt of Kush. Before I could lie and tell him I wouldn't deal with her, my phone rang. I excused myself to take the call. Carlton shot me a side-eye; he saw it was Alexis.

I walked away as I answered the phone, "Alexis, I have been calling you since you left my house. What the fuck is going on?"

"Wesley, it is so nice to hear from you. I'm sorry that I have a future husband who was pissed that I came home at four in the morning smelling like fresh soap."

"Can you get out tonight? I need to see you."

"Wesley, can I ask you a question? Did you send that nasty ass stripper to fuck Chase?"

"I would never hurt you, Alexis; that was all him." I lied. Hell yeah, I told her ass to fuck him. If he worried about someone else, then he couldn't focus on her ass. As a matter of fact, I told Camille's ass not to give up that easy either; she had to pull out every trick in book to get his attention. "So the white boy cheated on you, huh?"

"Yes, Wesley, he did."

"And you're going to stay with his ass?"

"I'm not discussing this with you."

"How long are you allowed to stay out?"

"As long as I want. I'm grown."

"Fine. See you at six and you are staying the night. It's Friday. You gotta let me cheer you up."

"I'm good, and no sex, Wesley."

She knew that she would give me that pussy. I had no idea why she was playing. I busted out laughing before saying, "Don't wear any panties, okay? And meet me at the strip club."

I knew her ass liked to see the stripers just as much as I did. She agreed and then hung up. Carlton stared me down as I walked back over there.

"Wesley, let me just tell you this. If I get caught in the crossfire, Imma shoot that bitch right between the eyes."

There was no need to respond to Carlton; if anything happened to Alexis, there was no rock he could hide under.

"I have a few cops on the payroll that will get back everything we lost. Come on, muthafuckas, we got shit to do."

ALEXIS

I had never been so happy to see the weekend. I was sad that I wouldn't wake up to Chase. Saturdays and Sundays were the days Chase and I spent time together. Usually I served him breakfast in bed wearing a thong and stilettos. Then we made love, took a nap, a shower, and then we went out on a date. Sundays, we went to church and then I would wash and iron his clothes. Last, we had dinner with his parents unless something came up with work. It worked for us.

On my desk was our engagement picture. As I looked at it, I started to cry. What did I do to make Chase cheat on me?

"Hey, Lexi, there was a shooting. We gotta hurry up so we can be first on the scene," my cameraman Michael called.

Slowly getting up from my desk, I joined Michael and we made our way to the car. Michael had become a good friend, we spent every moment together for work. Once we were in the car, he looked at me and said, "Spill it, and don't say 'ain't nothing wrong' because you look like shit, Wesley sent you flowers and you haven't talked to Chase all day."

"Damn, we need to get yo ass a woman, so you can stay out of my fucking business." I laughed before saying, "The short version—two days ago, I had sex with Wesley. Came home at four a.m. and Chase lost it. On my way home, I saw that bastard Chase with a stripper. Turns out Chase has been fucking her. He met her at that party y'all went to… So, I left him."

"Damn, girl, that's crazy. Do we need to fuck up the lieutenant? How dare his ass cheat on you. With yo fine ass, you need to quit playing and let me hit that," he replied, cracking up.

"If you only fucked just women."

Michael was cute as a button, a little overweight, but had nice caramel skin, and light brown eyes. He always had my back and if I told him, he would beat the fuck out of Chase. He was the brother I never had and I loved him to death. The only issue with him was he played both sides of the field. He had a live-in girlfriend Toni, but he also had a man Marcus. It wasn't an issue; that shit was just weird as fuck.

"Michael, I need a huge favor. I need you to follow Chase, see if he's still fucking her," I pleaded. Michael shot me the side-eye then he halfheartedly agreed.

"I told you his ass wasn't what you made him out to be. And yes, bitch, you can crash at my house. Toni won't mind looking at your sweet ass. I think she has a crush on you."

We made it to the crime scene where a thirteen-year-old boy had been shot. Some random act of violence. Lo and behold, Chase was there. He was the last person I wanted to see. My cameraman saw the look I shot his ass, and smiled. Chase's eyes burnt a hole in me as I did my follow-up interviews with the crime scene witnesses. He watched my every move. Every time he tried to approach me, someone distracted him. I bet that was the work of Wesley. Oh well, fuck him. He had violated, and this pussy that he craved was off limits.

WESLEY

I pulled up on the scene, knowing Chase would be there. Yeah, I was being an asshole. I wanted him to know I was still working Alexis' ass like an eight-hour graveyard shift. I saw the fear in her eyes as I appeared, the hate in his as everyone on the crime scene looked at me like I was the neighborhood superstar. My appearance was necessary.

I was Louis V down to my necklace with the Louis V emblem. I watched as Chase gawked at my red 2016 BMW coupe. I did like the other onlookers. I watched as they bagged and tagged the young bull. Damn, I wondered who the fuck shot him. Someone would pay for taking this kid's life. These streets loved no one.

I made my way to the crowd and noticed that Alexis watched my every move. I stepped towards the victim's mother so that I could embrace and console her. Every eye in the crowd seemed like it was transfixed on us. I knew her son; he was a runner for me. As I freed her from the embrace, knowing all eyes were on me, I put two stacks in her hand to cover any expenses. I told her if she needed anything else to hit me or Carlton up.

As I turned to leave, the crowd parted like the Red Sea. I smiled as I walked through the crowd. I pissed him off, making her ass crave me even more. I sat in my car as I watched Chase shoot a fuck-you expression my way. I just smiled as I drove away.

I had to get things ready for Alexis. She loved lingerie so I had one of my girls pick up one of each item in her size. I loved heels so I had them get those too. Her ass also had a sweet tooth. She would eat snacks all damn day long. I got this bitch I fuck who owns a bakery, so she hooked a nigga up. Tonight, I would get my queen back.

I ordered flowers for her and got some ingredients for chicken and broccoli.

I texted her.

"Are we still on?"

"Yes."

"Change of location. My house."

I waited for her to respond back talking shit, but simply said, "Okay."

Yes, now I needed to run some errands before I could get dinner started.

CHASE

I see I'm going to have to turn up the heat on his cocky, disrespectful ass.

The way people treated him, like he was some hood savior, knowing all the time he created the chaos. I got something for his ass; I knew he was the dick that Alexis was crying on. Her ass looking at his ass like how a fat kid looked at a fresh-baked cake. I knew his punk ass pulled that whole stunt for me, but he didn't realize he was burning time with me. Earlier in my career, I took bribes from the Russians but he had me fucked up if he thought he would keep disrespecting me.

Alexis was always beautiful but today she looked tired. I tried to see her a few times and people kept asking me stupid-ass questions. I missed her ass like crazy. Sadly, I had been spending time with Camille. Every time I got home, her ass was at my door half naked, trying to suck my dick. I told her ass last night was the last fucking time. And she said okay. When I got home, her ass better not be waiting for me to get off.

***

I interviewed over twenty people that knew shit about what happened to that kid. I told one of my officers that we would need to talk to Wesley and his crew. I knew that kid was a runner for him. What type of man put innocent kids in harm's way? It was a long day. I was hungry and tired as fuck, not to mention I just wanted to go home, eat dinner, and talk to Alexis. When I got home, Camille was standing on my porch and Alexis was pulling up.

"Fuck me," I screamed.

I walked to Alexis' car so that I could explain what was going on.

"Really, Chase?" she screamed.

"No, babe, it isn't what it looks like."

I tried to calm down Alexis when Camille strolled her ass off the porch talking shit.

"Chase, why is this bitch here? I thought you took out the trash," Camille said with a lot of attitude.

"Did this nasty-ass stripper just call me trash? Bitch, you use your pussy to make money and not your brain, but what you should do is shut your fucking mouth," yelled Alexis.

"Bitch, I won't shut my mouth. What the fuck are you going to do if I don't shut my mouth?"

I saw this shit happening before I could even grab Alexis. She knocked the shit out of Camille. Her body fell to the ground and Alexis straddled her, beating the shit out of her. After a few moments, I grabbed Alexis, who then attacked me. It was a struggle trying to retain her ass but finally, I wrestled her to the ground. She tried to kick me, I didn't want to hurt her. I just wanted her to calm the fuck down. Eventually, she did calm down.

"Get off me, Chase."

"Only if you relax."

"I'm good."

I let her up and she hopped in her car and she left. *Damn it.*

I helped Camille off the ground and she said, "I came by to tell you that I'm pregnant."

I'm officially fucked.

ALEXIS

I couldn't believe that Chase had that bitch at my house and she wanted to run her mouth. She had me fucked up and so did he. All I wanted to do was see him. Oh my fucking God, I could set his ass on fire right now. I got to my hotel room and got a text from Wesley saying to come to his house.

There was no reason to even fight it. I lost the man of my dreams to some stripper. I had to relax so I took a nice, hot bath, and drank a bottle of wine. Before I knew it, an hour had past and I needed to get dressed so I could go see Wes. Once out of the bathtub, I found a form-fitting red dress. I put on a bra but no panties. I decided to have two more glasses of wine. I couldn't believe that Chase was no better than Wesley. How in the fuck did I end up falling for two sorry-ass men? I thought getting a white man would be better than the black ones that I had in my life. All men were the fucking same and I would treat them the way they have treated women for years.

I would use them to get a nut or two. I laughed to myself. I threw my hair in a ponytail. It would be easy for Wesley to pull or play in whatever he decided to do tonight. I called for an Uber. There was no point in me trying to drive; I had been drinking. Twenty minutes later, the Uber had arrived and the driver was cute. He told me how he loved watching me on TV and asked me for my autograph. I gave him my number instead. He smiled from ear to ear.

Awww, I thought, a man was never that excited to be around me. I got out of the Uber, making my way to Wesley's door. While standing at the front door, the aroma of food filled my nose. I had no idea what he was cooking, but it smelled great. I knocked on the door and waited for him to open it. Instead, he yelled, "It's open." I walked in to see him stirring pots. I loved a man that could cook. He had flowers and treats sitting on the table.

"It smells great in here."

"Thank you, babe."

Instead of having a seat at the table, I hopped on the counter. I opened my legs, showing him my freshly shaved pussy. He chuckled, moved the pots off the stove, and then gave me his full attention.

"I figured that we would skip dinner and go straight to dessert." I replied.

He stepped between my legs, dropping his pants. When he was close to me, we kissed, allowing our tongues to do the forbidden tango. Our tongues made a sweet song. In that moment, I was lost in the kiss and all I needed was to feel him inside of me. He moved from kissing my mouth to my neck. I helped him out of his pants. His dick stood at attention. He pulled my dress up so that he could enter me and when he did, I took in a deep breath as his manhood filled my insides. A moan escaped my lips as I entered the wonderful world of passion. For the first time in years, I felt like Wesley was making love to me.

"Alexis, is this pussy mine?" Wesley whispered.

I said the thing that all women would say, "Yes." I hope that wasn't a huge mistake.

WESLEY

I sat here watching Alexis as she lay sleeping. *What the fuck have I gotten myself into?* I must admit this pussy really had me doing stupid shit. I would never go against Carlton's word for anybody but Alexis had a nigga's head fucked up. I should've left her ass alone. It was amazing how innocent, and beautiful she looked. I headed into my man cave to smoke a blunt to clear my head.

I knew Chase would do whatever it took to lock my ass up by all means so he could have Alexis to himself. Yeah, he would give her a pass on me knocking the bottom out of that pussy because he fucked up as well. I understood where he was coming from.

Sorry, back to me, I got to put some distance between us. Alexis used me to piss Chase off, to get the fucking she deserved. It wasn't love for me; it was just to piss Chase off. We both were each other's Achilles heel. I could take Alexis from him like he could take my freedom away from me. I heard Alexis moving around so I made my way back to the bedroom. She sat in the bed, looking at her cell phone when I came back into the room.

"Hey, sleeping beauty."

She looked up at me, giving me a soft smile that didn't really hit her eyes. She looked like she had a lot of shit on her mind. I got in the bed next to her.

"Alexis, is this real?"

"Is what real?"

"This with us or are you just using me to make Chase mad? If you are, this is a dangerous game that you are playing."

"I love you, Wes. I have loved you for as long as I can remember, but we want different things."

"Your white boy is turning up the heat on us. You need to put a stop to it before I have his ass marked."

"Wesley, the only way he will leave you alone is if I go back to him and if I do that, then you won't have me."

"Fuck it. I will kill that cracker then."

"Let me figure out a way to handle him."

We didn't say anything else about him. I made love to her for the rest of the morning and told her to meet me back here later. She kissed me before taking a shower and leaving.

****

I sat on my couch sipping some Cognac, puffing on some pineapple Kush. I laughed to myself, knowing Carlton would put a slug in my ass if he knew I was still fucking Alexis. Just as I was refreshing my drink, there was a knock at the door. I set my drink down on the bar and made my way to the door. I got excited as I swung the door open to be met by Chase with his gun drawn. He rushed me with his 9mm pointed at me.

"Where the fuck is she?" he roared.

I smiled then sneered, "Would you like a drink?"

Chase looked like a man possessed.

"Why are you fucking me?" he growled as he pressed the barrel of the gun in the center of my chest.

I grabbed the barrel, then grimaced. "Muthafucka, are you serious?"

Chase flinched at my response.

"You running up in my shit looking for Alexis, pulling out your gun. Get the fuck out of here," I laughed.

The fact that I was taking him so lightly only pissed him off. He took the gun and smacked me across my face. I grabbed my face as I tasted blood in my mouth. I rushed his ass, knocking him off balance. The gun slid by the front door. I pinned his white ass down. I hit him with a flurry of jabs to his face. He winced in pain as his face was now discolored from my blows.

"Get the fuck out of my spot," I spat as I yoked his ass up by his collar.

"This shit isn't over," he yelled as I dragged his ass to the door. I slung his gun out the door. I knew he was in a bad head space. As he cleared my doorway, Alexis was pulling up. I stood in the doorway as he was trying to get his wits about him after the ass-whooping I had just laid on him.

"What the fuck are you doing here?" he yelled in Alexis' direction as he propped himself on his car.

Alexis looked in his direction, rolling her eyes. "Chase, go home to Camille. We're done."

"Chase, right now you're trespassing. Do I need to call 911?" I teased as he watched Alexis hug me.

"This shit is not over, Wesley, believe that," he threatened.

"Chase, just leave," agreed Alexis. I held my phone in the air, play dialing 911.

"You're lucky if I don't press charges on your ass," I assured him.

His face was black and blue.

"Alexis, get your ass home or you will regret it," he scowled.

"Would you like something to drink?" I asked Alexis as I couldn't take my eyes off how her dress looked like it was painted on her ass.

"I would love a drink."

We walked into the house and I took out a glass. Last night she was ready to fuck so she didn't get to open her gifts. After I offered a glass of wine, I got her stuff from Victoria's Secret.

Alexis took the whole glass of wine to the head. I could tell that she was stressed out.

"Wes, after our talk this morning and now seeing Chase acting crazy, there is only one thing left to do. That's for me to make things right with him. We could still mess around. I just don't want you to end up in jail because of me."

I fucking hated her plan but she was right. If I kept fucking her, Chase would arrest me. I also knew that once her mind was made up, there was no changing it.

For real, I think that I'm going to have to kill that fuck boy.

CHASE

I hit the steering wheel out of frustration. I really fucked up. I looked in the mirror at my battered face. I dabbed a handkerchief on my busted lip, pissed that I gave Wesley the upper hand in this situation. Rash thinking wasn't a good choice. If he really wanted to be an asshole, he really could file charges on me. I literally did trespass and flashing a gun only amplified the situation. Alexis had me all kind of fucked up. Camille's presence wasn't helping any. I had to get rid of her ass; she had become a liability. I, like her, had taken an ass whooping the other day, then she said that she was pregnant. Then she asked to crash at my place for a few days and I agreed.

I pulled into my driveway aggravated, not really wanting to deal with Camille's annoying ass. I cut my headlights off, coasted into my driveway to get my thoughts together. I saw her ass peeking out of the curtains, I sighed. Yeah, it was time for her ass to go. I needed time to think. I knew with Camille around, that wasn't about to happen.

Alexis had it fucked up if she thought I would let her go that easily. I would let Wesley breathe for a minute until this blew over. I got in the house and there was no dinner done and Camille's few items were all over my couch. I wasn't used to coming home to this shit. Alexis always had the house clean and dinner done. A few seconds later, I lost my shit. I pulled my gun out on Camille. She started crying, begging me not to kill her, saying it was all Wesley's idea. She really was pregnant and it could be mine, but she wasn't sure. She had sex with a few other men.

I guess I wasn't the only one playing a dirty-ass game, but as soon as Alexis heard that it was a setup, she would have to forgive me.

"Look, Camille, I need you to get the hell out and we have to have some type of blood test for that baby. I have some friends that can get that taken care of asap. If and only if it is my baby, then I will take care of the baby, but I won't take care of you. You can never approach Alexis again, do you understand?"

"Yes, I understand, Chase."

She got her shit and left. I was so stressed out I just lay on the couch and went to sleep. I woke up the next morning to ice water being poured on me. I hopped up and it was Alexis. I was happy to see her ass.

"We need to talk." I said.

"That's why I'm here. I need you to leave Wesley alone. I'm willing to come back to you if you promise to leave him alone. Don't put him in jail because you're mad about me."

"He had Camille seek me out and seduce me. I'm supposed to be cool with that?"

"You stuck your dick in that bitch. You were supposed to have self-fucking-control. So anytime a bitch throws you pussy, you just gonna take it? What do I mean to you, Chase? When you love someone, you don't hurt them."

"Alexis, I'm sorry. I don't know what came over me with Camille, but it's over. I only want to be with you. I miss you so much. Please come back home."

"Before I agree to come home, I want you to give me your word that you will leave Wesley alone."

Even though I would tell Alexis that I would leave Wesley alone, I wouldn't. He set me up and I would make his ass pay, especially if Camille was pregnant. I knew that I willingly fucked her, but if he wouldn't have told her to fuck with me, none of this shit would've happened. Not to mention I hated that black son of bitch and he would fall for this shit. I would just have to go about it a different way.

"Alexis, there is something that I have to tell you."

"What?" she snapped.

"Camille is pregnant."

"Wow, Chase, I'm supposed to marry you but you have the next bitch pregnant."

"I'm sorry, babe. I really fucked up, like really, really. I'm sorry."

"Fuck this, Chase. How would you feel if I was pregnant with another man?"

She had a good point. If she told me she was pregnant with another man's baby, I'd kill him and her and I'd get away with it too.

"Alexis, I'm sorry. Shit got out of control. I promise to make it up to you."

Alexis didn't say anything at all. She just rose and left. If she went to Wesley's house, I would put a bullet in his head.

ALEXIS

After leaving Chase, I needed to have a drink. I typically would go to one of Wesley's clubs but not tonight. I wasn't in the mood for his smug attitude, not to mention I didn't want to be drinking and driving. Since I decided not to stay with Michael and Toni, I headed to the hotel. Once inside, I went straight to the bar.

As soon as I sat down, I ordered a double shot of white label Scotch and a Coke chaser. Threw back my shot followed by the Coke. I ordered another shot and some plain chicken wings.

My phone rang and it was Mr. Cocky also known as Wesley. Even though I wasn't in the mood to talk to him, I answered.

"Yes."

"Your white boy is in my club looking for your ass." I knew the foul ass would come looking for me, but fuck him.

"Throw his ass out," I fumed.

"I can't beat his ass again. He might press charges." I laughed. "Where are you?" fumed Wesley like he was my man.

"I'm around," I shot back. I could tell my response wasn't one he wanted to hear but he was a big boy. He would get over it.

"That smart-ass mouth is going to get you fucked up," scuffed Wesley.

I wasn't in the mood for his ass either.

"So, you called me about Chase?" I questioned him, not giving five fucks.

"For real, I know what you are going through but reel that shit in. I'm not the one."

The alcohol had kicked in so I just ended the call as I went back to tending to my drink. These niggas got me fucked up. I wished Wesley would put hood hands on me. I would kill that son of bitch.

Just that fast, I had drifted down memory lane. Remembering my mother standing in the kitchen as my father approached her, reaching his arm all the way back, smacking her. Her frail body flew across the floor. I was ten when that happened and I knew then that I would never turn into my mother. I would kill a muthafucka before I let him kick my ass.

WESLEY

I knew her ass didn't just give me the dial tone. What the fuck? I would have to fuck her and this white boy up. As I walked back into the club, Carlton pulled me to the side.

"Yo, cuz, wassup with the narco in here? I thought you told me that you weren't fucking with Alexis anymore," inquired an agitated Carlton.

I looked at his ass sideways, and then replied, "Cuz, you know he's fucking with Camille. Calm down."

Carlton knew that I had just shot him part of the truth. He just frowned and walked off.

"Cuz, handle that shit. We don't need them problems."

"For the record, that pussy got you fucked up. Cause I see you lying for it."

"I ain't lying. He is fucking with Camille."

Although Alexis was the real reason why he was here. She must not be talking to him and he felt the need to bring his ass out to our club, thinking she would come through. His punk ass sat over in the corner stalking my shit like he owned it. What kept me from putting a bullet in his brain was Alexis. She would never talk to my ass again. Then again, she had let me fuck her three times. I laughed to myself as he sported the remnants of the ass whooping I gave him proudly. Finally, I took my ass to my office and texted Alexis.

"Yo ass better not hang up on me again. I'm not that white boy."

"Fuck you, Wesley."

"You have fifteen minutes to get here before I have three bullets put in his fucking head."

"Do whatever the fuck you have to do. Now leave me the fuck alone."

She was really testing my patience, I swear she must not value his life or hers. Alexis must want to get fucked up. She thought I couldn't get to her ass, but I always knew where to find her ass. When we used to date, I put a tracker on her phone. In the street life, one had to protect his woman and the tracker ensured that she was all right. She never knew that it was on her phone; it was a hider app. I linked us up and ten minutes later, I knew exactly where to find her ass. I must put her ass in line or she wouldn't disrespect me anymore. I grabbed my suit jacket, left Carlton a note, and left out the back door. I didn't want that white boy following me, trying to cause me problems. Just in case he put one of his pig friends on me, I cleaned out my car, making sure it was drug and gun free.

ALEXIS

Damn, I couldn't enjoy my drink with folks coming over into my space. Yes, I was on the news but no, I didn't want you all in my face. I slid from the bar into a darkened corner to drink in peace. I had a lot going on with Wesley, and Chase's punkass. I was pissed at Wesley for setting him up, but madder at Chase for taking the bait, and getting a strip club whore pregnant. Nothing against her, he was responsible for his actions. The fact still stood that her ass was pregnant. Plus, Wesley thought he was slick trying to act interested now that Chase wanted to marry me.

Sex with Wesley was amazing and Lord knew that my body missed his touch and now my pussy craved him. Hell that was the last of my issues. What in the hell was I supposed to do now? How dare Chase fuck that bitch raw, like he didn't know that she could get pregnant? His ass must think I'm Boo-Boo the fool, as I took my shot of Scotch to the head. Wesley was full of shit too. I knew he only wanted me just to piss Chase off. The bar was getting crowded with onlookers so I knew I would have to take this party to my room. I was a public figure so getting white boy wasted wouldn't be a good look for me. I rose up from my corner table to exit the bar before anyone noticed me. As I was about to go out the exit, I felt a tug at my jacket. I quickly turned around, only to be face to face with Carlton.

"Hey, lady it's been a minute," he smiled, showing his perfect-aligned pearly whites.

Caught off guard, I stammered, "Yes, it has been." I smiled because I knew Carlton was on some crazy shit.

"So, I heard you're getting married?" pried Carlton.

I paused before answering, just wanting to get to my room.

"Yeah, in the fall if God's willing," I lied as I saw three guys walk up behind him. I hurriedly said, "Well, it was nice seeing you."

But, his facial expression darkened as he picked up on me trying to leave. One of the guys moved closer.

"So, your fiancée cool with you fucking my cousin?" spat Carlton.

I was speechless at his question. I responded, "Last I remembered, Wesley and I were grown," as I rolled my eyes.

"Watch your fucking mouth when it fucks with my money," fumed Carlton, now pointing at me.

Just that quick, he went from zero to messy. I started to walk away when one of the guys blocked my path.

"Excuse me, please," I said, but he didn't budge.

I whipped around to face a smiling Carlton.

I rolled my eyes, now aggravated, "Can you get your goon?" but he continued to smile.

"Can you stop fucking my cousin?" he responded.

"Look, Carlton, I told Chase to leave y'all alone. I would never fuck with y'alls money."

"Why the fuck was he looking for you in my fucking club?"

"You need to ask him that. Last time I checked, I'm not him. Or ask that stripper bitch that's pregnant with his baby. Now leave me the fuck alone."

As those words left my mouth, Wesley walked up. He noticed the uneasy look on my face.

"Lex, you good?" he questioned, looking concerned but pissed at the same time.

"Carlton wants us to stop fucking. He ruined my alone time. This is all your fault. You sent that slut after Chase and now Chase wants a war."

"Tony, take Alexis to her room." Wesley calmly barked at the man blocking me.

He finally spoke, "C'mon, let's go. You heard Wesley."

I looked at Wesley and sighed, "I'm a big girl. I don't need an escort."

"Alexis, can you do what the fuck I ask for once?" Wesley snapped.

Rolling my eyes, I walked away feeling like a prisoner. I purposely stumbled to draw his attention as Wesley went to the bar. Tony shadowed me.

"Ma'am, are you okay?" he asked as I caught my balance

I answered, "Yes, I just lost my balance, that's all." I giggled.

"Oh, my God. You're Alexis on the spot," he gushed.

I threw my hands up and smiled, "Guilty as charged."

"Well, you have a good evening," I chimed as I saw the coast was clear.

"You as well," he smiled.

I let out a sigh of relief. Minutes later, I collapsed on my bed, shocked at Carlton. He had never said more than a few words to me in the past.

I had never been so happy to see Wesley in my life. I was still in a drinking mood so I went to my mini-bar to see what I had on hand. I grabbed the mini bottle of Hennessy, and I dropped some ice cubes in my glass. I gulped it down and let out a hearty gasp from the burn. I was looking at the bar deciding what I would drink next when there was a knock at the door. I sighed, grimaced my face as I made my way to the door. I looked through the peephole but didn't see anyone. So, as I turned on my heel to revisit the bar, a knocking sounded again at the door. I stormed back to the door, and this time I snatched it open, aggravated.

"Hey, beautiful," smiled Wesley.

He wore a chocolate suit, with a blue button down, brown and blue tie, with some crocodile-skinned boots. His perfectly aligned teeth almost blinded me. I was speechless that he had found out where I was. He extended his hand, holding a dozen red roses. Where the fuck did he get roses from? I damn sure didn't see them when we were at the bar.

"What are you doing here?" I whined, knowing my body was craving him. I was floored at his persistence. For him to have roses this late, I was impressed.

"So, can a brother come in?" he smirked as I smelled the fresh-cut roses.

"I hope you checked your cousin."

He pushed past me. Coming into the room.

"Yeah, I did."

"Good," I said, tossing my body in the bed.

"Let's get in the Jacuzzi," he suggested.

"No, Wesley. I don't want to get in the Jacuzzi." I repeated my statement again, trying to convince myself that statement was true.

Wesley paid no mind to what I had said; he walked into the bathroom and turned on the water.

"I'm not taking a bath with you."

Wesley turned the water off and I turned to walk away, not really sure where the fuck I was going. He grabbed a fist full of my hair, forcing me back to him. As he stood behind me, I took in his scent.

"Bend over," he commanded as he helped me to bend. He pushed his dick into me. I let out a moan. He pounded himself inside me over and over. This was his way of making me submit. Everything was about control with Wesley. I was tense but after a few moments, I threw my hips back, enjoying the pounding that he gave me. We were having a fight with our bodies, but I was losing. He pulled my hair a little harder and I came all over his dick, screams escaped my lips. He kept pounding, my legs got weak and unstable. Finally, he released his seed.

"Now let's take that bath."

This time I complied. We got in the tub and I lay my head on his chest, finally relaxing and remembering all the reasons why I fell in love with him to being with.

Chase would've never fucked me into submission.

CAMILLE

I sat here looking at Chase's weak ass as he was drunk again. He was all fucked up over Alexis fucking Wesley blatantly. What his dumb ass didn't know was this was Wesley's baby. I ran interference for Wesley so he could get with Alexis; he paid me well to be a distraction. Chase was a good guy when he wasn't stressed out about Alexis. But he was an asshole when he drank. When he told me I ruined his life, I responded by telling him his dick ruined his life. When I met him at his friend's bachelor party, I knew then he was lame but the bands Wesley paid me made Chase sexy as hell to me.

Some of the bitches in here thought I was a hoe. This hoe was getting her muthafucking coins. So, I would be a hoe if I got fifteen grand in the bank and I managed to break up a happy home while another nigga paid my bills and one bought me clothes. Why they were just shaking their ass, I was stacking my paper, so fuck all them bitches.

I learned at a young age that a fat ass would get me somewhere. My mom didn't want me so my grandmother worked long hours. When she wasn't at work, she had me all in church. Assistant Pastor Greg took it upon himself to have his way with me. He only had to force himself on me once before I learned that it was easier to do what he wanted. Soon I realized that since I had the pussy I had the power. Greg went from the predator and he became the prey. He thought that I was all in love with him when I was just using him for all the stuff he gave me. Then I met Sam. I was sixteen and Sam was twenty-four. He had a nice car and he always threw money like most dope boys did. He also had a woman but I wasn't worried about that bitch. She had to worry about me. She didn't even see me as a threat. I could see why she was so pissed when she came home to find her nigga eating my pussy. I remember that shit like it was yesterday.

She had seen us together and he said she was just his best friend. She didn't trip. A few weeks later, he and I were talking about how his back game was strong. I said let me find out you slinging good wood. We constantly flirted, that led to us fucking on a regular basis. Yeah, I had played second best, but it always benefited me in the long run. I could've given five fucks about his main women. I was in it for the money.

Every side bitch had a backstory and I had mine. I shook my ass for cash, but it was what the fuck it was. Eventually, I would get my man. Wesley and I had a connection. I knew he thought that he wanted Alexis. But I planned to get that bitch out of his system. I thought that I had him, but he needed a little more time to see she wasn't shit.

I had to admit that I was pissed off when he asked me to fuck Chase, but Wesley wasn't the type of man to say no to. Men like him preferred submissive women. I played the part. Once again, I was hurt when I told him that I was pregnant and he ultimately said get rid of it. Then he said hold off on it so I could use it to break up Chase and Alexis. Once again, I did what I was told. Hopefully, this would be the last time he asked me to do him a favor. The pay was great but I wasn't into white men. Plus, Chase's sex game sucked; he had little dick syndrome.

I sat at the bar waiting for Wesley to come back to the club, but he never showed up after waiting three hours. Carlton finally sat at the bar, looking aggravated. He smelled so fucking good I couldn't help but to take in his aroma. I gave him a smile as he ordered two double shots of Jack. As soon as the bartender set them on the table, he took the shots to the head. He ordered two more. I took it upon myself to massage his shoulders. He was so tense.

"Carlton, do you need to release some stress?"

"Yeah, bitch, let's go to the VIP room so that you can suck my dick."

"No, thank you, Carlton. I was just gonna give you a full body massage."

He jumped up and grabbed me by the arm, pulling me to the VIP room. He dropped his pants then sat down in the chair.

"I won't ask your ass again. Suck my dick."

"Wesley wouldn't like it if I gave you head."

"Bitch, you think that nigga gives a fuck about you?"

"I know that he does."

He burst into laughter.

"He loves you so much he pimped your ass out. Do you think that he would let Alexis fuck another man? I mean, really. Where do you think he is right now?"

He killed my feelings, but I would never let him do that.

"What do I get out of sucking your dick?"

He pulled his gun out and said, "To live another day."

My feet were planted and my body couldn't move. This may be what people meant when they said scared stiff. He waved his hand up and another girl came in with two more drinks. As she was about to walk out, he said, "How about you bitches give me a show. I want some girl-on-girl action."

He had to pick one of my biggest haters to ask me to fuck.

"Carlton, I won't touch that bitch at all."

"Fine, then lay down and let the bitch eat your pussy."

I pulled off my dress, exposing my baby blue matching bra and panties set. She followed suit. We looked at each other. She wrapped her arms around me, taking off my bra. She sucked on my breast and I had to admit that shit felt wonderful. I was into it way more than I thought I would. I whispered in her ear and she let my breath go. I removed my panties and we walked over to Carlton. I dropped to my knees and took his average-sized dick in my mouth. I sucked him as she sucked my pussy.

She hit all the right spots, giving me pleasure that no man had ever given. Damn, I couldn't believe that I really liked this bitch eating my pussy. The more she turned me on, the deeper I took his dick in my mouth. I moaned and was all into the moment. He pulled my hair and the bitch sucked my pussy and played with my ass. As she brought me to my climax, I played with his balls, giving him all the pleasure that I was getting.

He pushed my head away when he was about to nut, only to release in my face. What a disrespectful piece of shit. He commanded that the other girl lick it off. Next, he wanted her to ride my face. I refused, which didn't work out in my favor. He smacked the shit out of me, then decided that he would fuck me in the ass. Usually I'm all for anal, but he got pleasure out of hurting me. He sweetened the deal by having her eat my pussy. Tonight, pleasure was pain and my ass enjoyed every moment of it. Finally, I let her ride my face and pussy had a sweet taste. I got lost in her juices, enjoying every ounce of it. I sucked her dry then got her back wet again. I loved it. After a while, she and I had all the fun, leaving Carlton out. He just came and joined in the fun.

Once we were done, I hit the shower. Taking my ass to see Chase, he didn't act happy to see the mother of his child. Once I was in the house, I flopped on the couch.

"Look, Camille, I want you to get an abortion. I can't have you, that baby, and Alexis. That baby has to go. I will pay for everything. I will give you two thousand dollars and we become strangers. Do you understand?"

"Our baby's life is only worth two thousand dollars?"

"I don't even know if it's my baby, so let's be real. I'm being very generous," he spat.

"That's fucked up. But you know what? Imma do it. Then we will be strangers. I tell yo punk ass one thing—you will be back begging me to fuck your ass again."

"Yeah, yeah, yeah, now get the fuck out," he fumed.

He had already packed a couple of items I had here in a bag. Damn, he was serious. Wesley was gonna be pissed off.

What Camille wouldn't do was beg a nigga to stay in her life. Not now and not ever, fuck that white son of bitch. Okay, yeah. I was pissed off. I dumped men, they didn't dump me. What the fuck was this? As soon as I got outside, I flattened every one of his tries. Then started to bust the windows out of his car. He ran outside. Looking like a fucking demon, I swore his eyes were red. I hopped in my car and got the hell out of there, calling Wesley to tell him what happened. He didn't answer but I knew he was with Alexis. I went to get a room.

But twenty minutes later, I arrived at the Belair Hotel crying my eyes out. I checked in, having composed myself. I knew that Chase wouldn't report the vandalism I did to his car; he didn't want anyone to know about me. I grabbed my room key. As I walked to my room, I thought of how Carlton had treated me, how his words about Wesley were nothing but the truth. I was just a pawn in his and Alexis' game. Something like a checkmate move by him. I and this baby, Chase was expendable. If Chase thought he was done with me, he was dead wrong. Wesley's ass wasn't off the hook either; he had played me as well. Thirty minutes later, I had taken my shower. I was now stretched out across the bed, pissed at how this shit was playing out. I reached for my purse; I needed the blunt I had rolled earlier. Fucking with a muthafucka like Wesley would have a bitch pulling her tracks out. Anyway, let me handle this and I would talk to y'all later on.

CARLTON

I would be glad when Wesley realized it was always bands over bitches. He got with these hoes, lost his damn focus. He knew we had too much to lose. I would take him as a loss before I went back to being broke. We ran every block of Charlotte from North Charlotte to West Blvd. But what pissed me off was bitches who flocked to his ass like flies to shit. Yet his ass chose to chase after the one bitch who he knew he couldn't have. The fact that she was engaged to Chase, he was sacrificing the whole organization. Wesley was like a brother to me; we had always taken care of each other since we were kids. My mother had died in a car accident; his mother Joyce had raised me like her own. Four years older, I always covered his ass. We grew up in Dalton Village, in a government apartment off West Boulevard. I learned every facet of the dope game there.

When Wesley was sixteen, he held down the front and back hole of our hood. My aunt Joyce was usually gone over her boyfriend, Sim's house. He turned me onto the game. Now the nigga was gone, stuck on stupid about a bitch. I should've put a bullet in her fucking head back at the Belair. I spared her ass because there were too many witnesses. For real, I would like to fuck that bitch once or twice. She was cute but I needed to know what the hype was. Her pussy must be sunshine. She got two niggas ready to go to war about her ass. Yeah, Chase's white ass was a mark on my list too.

I headed to see his ass right now. I pulled up to his house and someone did a number on a car out front. Must have been a bitch. I would never understand why bitches got mad and fucked with a man's car. But I didn't understand bitches anyway. He sat on the porch. It was cold as a muthafucka out here and his stupid ass sitting on the car like it was ninety degrees.

He pulled his gun and aimed it at me. I got out of the car, holding my hands up.

"Chase, I come in peace."

"Why are you here?" he asked me.

"I'm here to talk," I responded.

"Well, speak then. I'm really not in a fucking mood," he mumbled as he still had his gun pointed at me.

"We have an issue," I said. "You are fucking with me because your bitch is fucking with Wesley. So, let me tell you how this shit is going to work. There is a tracker in Alexis' car and cell phone. If you keep fucking with me, I will have someone rape and kill the bitch. You need to call off your guards before she's dead as fuck, bro," I assured him.

"I spoke with Wesley and he is going to stop fucking her. I love money and there is no reason for us to be worked up over some pussy. I also know where the future Mrs. Manchester lays her head at night, so be smart."

Yes, I went to his house to threaten his bitch and his mom and that punk didn't say shit. He called me a few moments later and told me that I had a deal. I bet he had his friends checking on mommy. I told him to hold and I had someone shoot up the spot just to be a warning that I am not the one to fuck with.

This plan could go good or bad. My plan is for him to get the heat off us. He called right back.

"What?"

"You don't know who you are fucking with. Attack my family again and I will set all y'alls shit on fire, feds and all. Here's the deal. Tell Alexis to come home and marry me as soon as possible. Oh, yeah, and make Camille get an abortion and I will leave you alone," he warned.

"Wesley is another story. I will definitely be getting at him," Chase assured me.

"I talked to Alexis. She said that she would leave Wesley alone to save your life. So, you have no beef with him at this time," I told Chase.

"Carlton, why should I trust you?" questioned Chase.

I smiled, "Because I like bands over bitches. That is the Gucci Boys' motto. Wesley violated that creed, but we will handle him," I assured Chase.

"For real, Carlton. I have no issues with you. It's Wesley that's the problem. If you don't control him, then I will put him down like a rabid dog," spat Chase.

"Dude, your beef should be with your bitch. Can't nobody steal your bitch. She had the chance to walk away and the option to keep her legs closed. She willingly fucked Wesley. She is the one who's in the relationship with you, not Wesley," I fumed. "Chase, you sure you want to go this route? I mean it won't look good if it comes out you're having a baby by a black stripper," I teased.

"So, is that the best that you have?" he smiled.

"Well, let's see how you fare, seeing the locals love Alexis." I warned him.

I heard Wesley say that Chase was image conscious, which was a good way for me to get him on my side. He thought that him being with Alexis helped him get promoted quicker.

After a few moments of consideration, Chase agreed to my deal.

"I thought you would see it my way. For the record, just like you all keep files, records of us, we're doing the same. And this call was recorded." I smirked.

Chase didn't reply, which I assumed was good. I bet the cracker never thought that a hood nigga would outsmart his ass.

"Well, it's been a pleasure doing business with you," I teased.

The line went dead. That punk-ass bitch hung up on me. I laughed. Now I had to speak with Afon before any moves were made concerning Wesley. So for now, he got a pass.

Wesley's ass would never see me coming.

WESLEY

I had made love to Alexis all night and I woke up to Carlton blowing me up. I wanted to stay in Alexis' pussy all day, but I had to make moves. I had been distracted with this Alexis shit. Today, I had to deal with Elle; she was one of our top distributors but lately, the figures had been coming up short.

As I got dressed, I thought about how much I hated dealing with the Italians. Lately, they had been rampaging shit ever since their boss' son Miguel got killed. After that, their motto had been shoot first, ask questions later. Elle was over all dope operations, she ruled it with an iron fist.

I was dressed and peeped at Alexis lying in the bed. I admired her chocolate skin on the white sheets. Damn, my dick was getting hard. I wanted to be knee deep in her pussy but I had to go. Walking over to her side of the bed, I kissed her cheek. She didn't even move. I left her a note then rushed out the house.

As I pulled up to the security gate, the armed guard waved me in. I shook my head at how they had beefed up security. I hated being ass out by coming here solo; new faces who didn't know me always rubbed me the wrong way. I got a funny vibe when Elle greeted me. She was escorted by armed guard. I watched as they cooked, weighing the cocaine that was now crack. I rubbed my hands together, thinking about the money that would be made off the dope.

Our new hybrid Kush was already getting flooded through the projects. Elle watched overhead from a balcony as I took in the operation. She watched like a mother hen over her chicks in the farm yard.

I was excited at the possibilities of the money he would make off the drug haul. My mind raced at the fact that my greed had made me take out his best friend, brother, partner in crime Manuel in the process. I liked how Elle ran the Gucci Empire with an iron fist.

"Are you enjoying the show?" asked Elle.

"I love how you run your business," I smiled. "So, when do you think the first shipment will hit the streets?" I inquired.

"As we speak," Elle answered dryly.

"So, we're serving them as we speak?" I asked just as dryly.

Ellie's phone rang so she stepped away. I stepped closer so I could hear what she said.

"Hello, this is Elle?" she answered.

Seconds later, she screamed. "What the fuck is going on, Ortiz? Well, only thing we got going on is processing this weight. We've had an agreement for years as always. Is it Afon's dope? We don't need that type of heat at our doorsteps. Fuck. Okay, bye."

Elle returned back to the production room as I still took in the synchronicity of the operation, not noticing Elle had returned and signaled her goons to get me. My back was turned as I felt the gun barrel in my back. My body tensed as her goons clamped my neck to escort me out of the room, as Elle followed closely behind with another hired gun.

"What the fuck is going on? I don't know what the fuck y'all are trying, but I damn sho ain't with it," I fumed.

"Tell me where this dope came from, Wesley? Why the fuck would you bring drama to our house?" yelled Elle.

"I know you muthafuckas better put them damn guns at ease," I said.

"So, did you think you could bring dope to our house and walk away?" asked Elle.

The tension in the room thickened quickly as the goons' grips tightened on their guns.

"I'm going to give you two minutes to start talking. After that, it's out of my control," Elle assured me.

My body tensed at the thought of being fired on. I was usually the shooter. I now was the one who had death in my eyes, as one of the goons' gun was now planted at the back of my head.

"So, that's how we are going to do this?" I asked as he heard the gun cock.

Beads of sweat now covered my face. The gun exploded as it caught my earlobe and specks of blood scattered as I felt the heat of the bullet rip my flesh. I saw the light from the gun explosion.

"So, do you really want to do this?" commanded Elle as the gunpowder smell filled the room.

Blood trickled down my neck as streams of pain filled where the chunk of ear was; blood laid on the floor.

"So, talk or the next slug will be the showstopper. Did you really think you could pull this shit off?"

My neck was covered by blood that had soaked into my collar.

"I'm going to give you one minute to come clean or else," said Elle.

I took in the room and the blood-hungry goons who were itching to lay my ass down. I smiled, and put my hand in surrender to lighten the tension in the room. He knew I had to think quickly, as the second goon had lined up an infrared dot on my chest in a shooting stance. I put my hands up in surrender.

"I just got you a stay of execution," said Elle as she looked at me getting my ear tended to.

"No stay was needed; it was just a misunderstanding on both parts," I assured her as the nurse sewed what was left of my ear, I flinched as I responded and listened.

"Okay, I need to see your man Ortiz when this all is said and done," I barked.

"So, you're mad at him for doing his job?" asked Elle.

"At the time, his actions were justified."

I was now looking at the nub now a remnant of my ear, I grimaced as I did so. The goon responsible walked in. I jumped to my feet, and met him head on with a jab to his eye. An upper cut lifted him off his feet. I now hovered over him with his own gun pressed against his forehead.

"Muthafucka, tell me why I shouldn't body your ass."

Elle looked as the tempo of the room had changed quickly as her bodyguard who shot me had returned to the room. Elle took all the action in. Her guard lay on the floor, leaking blood. I was boiling mad as he lifted him by his collar and smacked the pistol against his face, making a loud thud with every strike.

"That is enough," yelled Elle as the medic who had attended to my ear now cowered in the corner. The other guard rushed in as he heard the ruckus going on in the room.

"Muthafucka, again tell me why I shouldn't kill you." I commanded. The second guard came in with his gun drawn as he burst into the room away from the production lab. Elle waved him to put the gun down and to remove his comrade.

Five minutes later, she had cleaners taking care of the mess. I, in a defensive mode, paced back and forth at the events that had unfolded today.

"What the fuck kinda shit you all got going on here?" I yelled.

Elle was unfazed by his angered demeanor.

"I don't know if you recognized it, but I have saved your ass today. A thank you would be nice."

"So calm your ass down. You would've done the same thing to protect your family." I looked at Elle with trust and desire. She did the same, in a standoff.

"Let's get this money and get over the bullshit," she mumbled as she made her way out of the room, back into the production lab.

"Go home and get cleaned up. We will get together later to discuss numbers. Celebrate our partnership," stated Elle.

"You owe me a fucking shirt, thanks to y'all bullshit," I barked.

"Get the fuck out of here," responded Elle jokingly.

I turned to leave to take in the view of Elle again. She wore a low-cut, form-fitting dress that made her ass look rounder. Her cleavage in the dress, plus her good push-up bra, made her tits look like a D-cup. She sported a bob cut, with piercing blue eyes.

My downfall was always a nice ass, a nice set of tits, which Carlton reminded me of often in the past when I did dumb shit behind a woman.

Five minutes later, I opened the door of my car. I sat for a minute to regain my composure. After today's events, I knew I had to make moves quickly.

"I can't believe this shit is unraveling so quickly," I murmured to myself as I exited the plant.

****

Back at Alexis' room…

I finished the meal that Alexis had waiting for me when she walked up behind me and ran her hand over my freshly cut head.

"Yeah, Daddy likes that," I closed my eyes and smiled.

Alexis pulled a knife from her back and put it on the right side of my head. I felt the cold steel meshing against my temple

"What the fuck you doing?" Alexis now had her other arm wrapped around my neck and bent over to whisper in my ear.

"Muthafucka, you better had been scoping out a job. If I find out otherwise, this knife will hack on your big ass."

I stood up with Alexis still holding onto my neck. I broke from her choke hold and said, "Are you out of your rabbit-ass mind?"

I now had lifted her off her feet, pressing against the wall. Her robe had become untied in the exchange, revealing her naked body. "I bet your big overgrown ass better put me down," she commanded as I had now hoisted her legs over my shoulders. Her pussy was directly in my face.

"I got your ass now," I joked.

She had her arms wrapped around my neck. I felt her wetness.

"I bet you better put me down," she smirked.

Knowing she loved when I manhandled her and even more when I ate the pussy, I now had her at an angle. Her hands rested on top of the mini-refrigerator while I had full access to the pussy. I slowly ran my tongue over her clit, slightly sucking on it. Pussy juice trickled down my hoodie.

"That's right, baby. Eat this pussy. You know what momma likes," she moaned.

As her nails dug into my shoulders, I now sped up the strokes as her hips gyrated at a steady pace.

"You going to make this pussy cum?" I now gently lay her on the kitchen table. As I sat down, I pushed her leg open as she lay naked, spread eagle. I slowly worked two fingers in and out of her pussy as I lightly sucked and licked her clit. Alexis yelled out.

"Oh, you black son of a bitch, you got this pussy cumming." Her body convulsed a few times and she collapsed. I lifted my head up, my face looking like it had been soaked in baby oil.

I just smiled and said, "You should get petty more often," as I made my way back to watch a movie.

CARLTON

I called Camille's stinking ass at least seven times before that bitch answered the phone.

"Hello," she said with an attitude.

"Camille, get rid of that baby. You need to tell Alexis that you were lying and you aren't pregnant with Chase's baby. Also, tell her that Wesley told you to sleep with him."

"Wesley will kill me."

"Bitch, I will kill you."

There was a silence on the phone. I could hear the bitch crying, acting like her ass was scared.

"Camille, I know that you have a mom and a sister. Oh yeah and that beautiful teenage niece Yawnha. Oh sweet, I wonder if she's a virgin. Maybe she would like to suck my dick. Should I ask her? Camille, should I have someone pick her up so I can do all types of bad things to her?"

"You nasty son of a bitch."

"Camille, I'm not playing with your stupid ass. Do what the fuck I say or you will have a front row seat to watch me fuck and kill the little bitch."

I hung up the phone.

Fear would motivate a bitch to do whatever I said. But just in case the silly bitch had second thoughts, I went to Concord High School. As soon as I spotted her, I walked up to her.

"Hey, Yawnha, I'm C. Your Aunt Camille asked me to pick you up."

"Ummm. No, thank you."

I walked closer to her, grabbed her by the arm, and said, "If you scream I will blow your brains out."

She started to cry as she walked to the car. I felt horrible. Ha, no I didn't. I put her in the backseat, making sure the child safety lock was on. Then I drove to a nice quiet spot.

Once we arrived at our location, I undressed her. Well, I just took off her shirt and pants, then took pictures and sent them to Camille from a burner phone, with the caption, "It's your move, bitch."

ALEXIS

I woke in the bed alone and with so much stuff on my mind, I still couldn't believe that Chase got that stripper pregnant. That shit pissed me the fuck off. I was a damn good woman and his ass should be proud to have me as his wife. Why wasn't I enough?

My thoughts were interrupted by a knock on my door. Who in the hell knew I was here? I got nervous as I thought about how it could be Carlton. He really hated me for some reason. I looked out the peep hole and it was that stripper bitch Camille. This bitch must want her ass beat.

She stood there staring at me. Her eyes were puffy; I could tell that she had been crying.

"Can I come in?" she asked.

"Only if you want your ass whooped again. Why the fuck are you here, bitch."

"Look, Alexis, we got off to a bad start. I only fucked Chase because Wesley told me to. He got me pregnant and told me to pin the baby on Chase. I did it because I love him and I thought that it would make him want me. This baby isn't Chase's."

I was speechless and furious with Wesley.

"Why are you telling me this?"

"Because Chase loves you and he's a good man."

How in the hell can I trust this bitch?

"Are you gonna have a DNA test just to be sure?" I questioned.

"No, I'm having an abortion," she cried.

Suddenly, I felt bad for her. I couldn't believe that Wesley would do that.

We talked a few more moments. Then she left and I got back in bed. As I lay there, my phone went crazy. Who was texting me? The number had an 850-area code, but it was pictures of Wesley with a white bitch. I literally felt steam coming out my ears. Just when I thought he had changed his ways. Who in the hell sent these photos? I was done being the bitch that he fucked. He better hope and pray I didn't kill his fucking ass. Tears formed in my eyes and steam came out my ears.

It was time to make up with Chase, I said as I got out of bed and hopped in the shower. After I was clean, I sent Chase a message telling him we needed to chat. I threw on a robe and ordered some lunch. Nothing fancy, just a steak and potatoes with a fresh garden salad.

It was a good thing that I ordered two. Wesley knocked on my door. I opened the door, shocked to see a bandage on his ear and his shirt covered with blood. He dashed to the shower and I found him something to wear. I was pissed with him, but I would wait before I checked his ass. He forgot that I was crazy as hell. But tonight, this muthafucka would see. He would know not to cross me ever again. I was tired of his bullshit. Sorry son of a bitch.

After his shower, Wesley sat at the table and started to eat his food. I grabbed the biggest knife I could find, rubbed his head, and then held the knife to his throat. We exchanged some words, but he didn't admit to being with another woman. Somehow, that talk led to him eating my pussy and I thought about how the fuck I would tell him that I was done with his ass.

I enjoyed every moment of it. Once he was done, we sat on the couch. There was no need to get dressed. I knew once I said I was done, he would try to fuck me.

"Wesley, can I ask you a question?"

"Yeah, babe, what's up?"

"Are you fucking with other women?"

"Hell, nah, this time it's just me and you."

I took my phone and threw it at his ass.

"Why did someone send me this? Pictures of you and some white bitch. That was the same shit you were wearing when you came in here. Oh yeah and Camille said that she was carrying your child and that you forced her to sleep with Chase?"

He was speechless. His nose flared and I could tell he was pissed.

"Wesley, I can't do this. I'm not gonna be the side chick. You play too many games, Wesley. I'm done with this shit. Please leave."

"Alexis, that white bitch is just the connect. We never fucked. I flirt because women like that shit. That's it and that's all. And Camille's ass is a fucking liar, I swear."

I rose from the couch, taking in a few breaths.

"Wesley, there will always be someone else with you. I can't do this anymore."

"Alexis, I will never let you go."

A river of tears flowed down my face. I expected Wesley to put up a huge fight but he didn't. He just left. I ran to the bedroom and cried. Finally, my phone rang and it was Chase. I had totally forgotten I told him I'd meet him. Now, I was three hours late.

"Sorry, sorry, babe. I have a bad headache and fell asleep. Can you just come to the Blair? I'm in Room 5203." I answered.

"Yeah, I'll be there. Give me twenty minutes,"

I got the phone, hopped in the shower, and threw on nice lingerie. The second shower helped me relax. Although I missed the hell out of Wesley, I knew that I couldn't continue this life.

Chase didn't miss a beat. Twenty minutes later, he was there smiling at me with some roses. We embraced. I had missed him, but sadly all of the emotions didn't rush back at once. All I could see was him with the stripper. But he was safe and that was what I needed right now. He sat down and we talked about when we would get married. We decided to just put a rush on it, so we would get married on Tuesday. Then we would have a big party and invite our friends. Not my idea of how I wanted to get married but hell, I didn't even want to get married given the situation and how fucked up things had been between us. Maybe it was the right thing for us to do.

We went to bed with no contact at all. We woke up the next morning and checked out of the hotel room. My mind was stuck on Wesley and how he could treat me this way. When I wasn't with Chase, I was thinking about him and when I wasn't with Wesley, I thought about him. The connection with me and Wesley was so real. And the sex was amazing. How would I live my life not being sexually satisfied by the man I love?

CHASE

Things were finally getting back to normal. Alexis was back at home in the bed next to me and life was great. In just twenty-four short hours, she would be Mrs. Chase Manchester. That had a ring to it. My baby would be my wife and man, was I excited. She didn't know that planned a party for us so as soon as we say our I dos, she would be surprised by all of our friends. I thought it would good because she had been kind of moping around the house pretending as if she didn't miss Wesley. But he was out of the picture. And thank God that crazy bitch Camille was out of the picture too. She got rid of that baby and had a talk with Alexis on my behalf, which was perfect.

She left me alone as I planned. There was nothing standing in the way of Alexis and me being together anymore. I looked at the clock. It was midnight and in ten short hours, I would marry the woman of my dreams. I had better get some rest. My phone began to ring just as I closed my eyes to go to night-night land. I really didn't want to talk to him, but he kept calling. Finally I answered.

"We need to talk, Chase," Carlton demanded.

"Today isn't a good day."

"This isn't optional, man. Get your ass here or I need to come there."

"Where the fuck are you? You know. I'm marrying Alexis in a few hours. I don't have time for this shit."

"Hey, listen. Don't your ass backpedal on me because I recorded our whole conversation," spat Carlton.

Fuck, these fucking monkeys were smarter than I thought. I was silent for a minute, knowing I had fucked up from making a deal with the devil.

"Chase, wassup? How are we going to handle this shit?" he growled.

I sighed, knowing I had to help his ass.

"How long can you sit on her body?" I asked.

"We need to handle this ASAP," he confirmed.

"I'm on my way," I sighed.

Five hours later, I woke a little bit late. It was time for me to make it down to the justice of the peace. I rose from my nap. Alexis was nowhere to be found. *Where the hell is she?* So I got up, brushed my teeth, washed my face. Picking up my cell phone, I called a couple of times but she didn't answer. What was she doing? I looked in the kitchen, the bathroom, on the mirror to see if she left me a message anywhere, but she hadn't.

Was this a case of the Runaway Bride?"

ALEXIS

I really didn't want to spend the rest of my life with Chase. The last two weeks had been miserable. I missed Wesley and everything about him, but he wasn't good for me. So, I had to move on, right? I tossed and turned for what seemed like hours, I just could not go to sleep. Finally deciding to get up, I needed to get some fresh air and a couple of drinks. In a couple hours, I would be Mrs. Chase Manchester and it might be one of the biggest mistakes of my life. My trip ended me at Wesley's establishment. *Alexis, what are you doing here? Why are you here?* Hopefully, I could slide in, throw back two shots, get back home, and everything would be perfect. Right? Wrong. Soon as I walked in the door, Wesley's goons were on me, pulling me up to his office. He was waiting in the chair with his arms folded, acting like he was some kind of black Godfather. He looked sexy. A part of me wanted to jump all over him. But I couldn't do this. I couldn't think about Wesley that way. I would be a married woman in a few short hours.

"Alexis, what are you doing here? Did you miss me that bad?"

"This is the only place I can have a drink without people recognizing me. Here, I'm just another girl."

"Alexis, we both know that you're more than just another girl."

"I'm shocked to hear you say that because to you, all I've ever been is just another girl."

"So, you came here tonight to bring his shoes to the table."

"No. I came here tonight hoping that I didn't see you and that I could have a drink and then I want to get back home. I'm going to be a married woman in a couple hours. I wanted some freakin' peace."

Wesley's face looked like he was about to throw up. His whole body language changed. Neither one of us said anything for a few moments. I could tell that my last statement totally caught him off guard. I felt bad that I was getting ready to move on with my life and be the number one woman in someone's life when I knew Wesley loved me and I loved him. Why couldn't love just be enough for him to say, 'Alexis, I'm going to let all of this go for you. We could run away, get married, and live La Vida Loca.' Right. In a case like this, you either conformed to his lifestyle, or walked away. He'd never change. I was too old for the women, the cars, the fast life, the drugs. I couldn't do it my heart, couldn't take it if he was dead. So there was no need for me to keep on pretending like I was cut out for this lifestyle. A part of me wanted to rush over and hug and kiss, and tell him that I was sorry. I would always be his. But I wasn't. I did what any other girl would do.

"Wesley, I have to go. It was a horrible idea for me to come here to have a drink. I guess the next time I need a drink I'll have to have one at home."

"Alexis, please stay a few moments and catch up. I miss you."

"It was a horrible idea for me to come here so I just better go. The last thing I need is for your crazy cousin telling Chase that he saw me here talking to you."

"Why would Carlton be saying to Chase anything like that?" he questioned.

"Well, I'm not a hundred percent sure why but I know that he and Carlton talk. I've heard them plotting, so honestly Wesley, you better watch your back. I don't think that Carlton has your best interest anymore. You were chasing too many bitches for him."

When he looked at me, his whole persona had changed. He went from sad to serious, and then he slammed his hand on the desk.

"I can't believe Carlton would cross me like that."

I walked over to him in an effort to console him. I touched his hand and said, "Wesley, why would I lie to you about this? I hundred percent know that Carlton has been talking to Chase. I don't know why and I don't know the extent of their relationship, but I do know that they talk. Last night, as a matter of fact, I heard him say something about Camille and I heard Chase say, 'I'm not going to deal with this right now.' So here's my question. Have you seen Camille tonight? Did she work tonight? If she's dead, why is your cousin calling my future husband instead of you? That's some shit to think about."

He looked at me and from his facial expression, he knew I was telling the truth. What I said made sense. Why were Chase and Carlton having conversations? Wesley took my holding his hand as a chance to grab me up and kiss me. I pulled back. I tried to fight it, but he just kept on kissing and finally, I was overtaken by the passion. We kissed and the next thing I knew, his hands were exploring my body, pulling up my dress. The moisture filled my secret place as he planted kisses down my neck, making his way down to my pussy. He had his face between my legs, then he pulled my panties off, threw them on the floor, and buried his face into my pussy, sucking, licking, and flicking his tongue.

This wasn't that bad if I just let him eat my pussy. Don't let him stick it in, but the next thing I knew, my dress was over my head and he entered me. Sweet baby Jesus. I missed him so much. I let out a moan as I wrapped my arms around him and started to work my hips. It was too late to stop now so I went with the flow. For the first time, it honestly felt like he made love to me. He did things we never did during sex. He let his guard down and stared in my eyes, telling me how much he loved me and he hated that he was about to lose me to another man.

The fact that he had claimed to have changed and to love me so much would typically make me want to leave Chase but I had heard this before. I couldn't fall back.

After we were finished, we lay on the floor in each other's arms. He looked at me and said, "Alexis, I know I've done a lot of shit and you shouldn't ever forgive me, but let me just make this one thing clear please. I love you. I've never loved anybody in my whole entire life. I always had to be the head gotta-make-money. I was taught to fuck bitches and make money. It was always different with you, Lex. This last time with you, I promised myself. I wouldn't fuck this up and I swear I've been true to you. I was fucking Camille, but that was before you. I swear I didn't get that bitch pregnant. Yeah, I did tell her to fuck Chase, but he could've said no. So can you really be mad at me?"

Damn, Wesley made a good point. Chase should've said no.

"Wesley, what about the white bitch?" I asked.

"And for real, the white girl, I didn't fuck her. Maybe I would've but it was only some sexual tension. I promise. I love you. Elle, the white bitch, that's all business. The bitch tried to kill me. Nothing pleasurable about it; the bitch tried to fucking kill me. That's what happened to my ear. I'm laying all my cards out on the table. I just want to be with you. I think you should marry Chase and after two or three weeks, we run away together. Spend our life together doing all the shit that we always planned when we were kids. I'm willing to give up this life for you, Alexis. I'll get out. I just can't get out and stay here."

Man, he didn't know how long I had waited for him to say those words to me. The only problem was I wasn't sure if I could trust it. Wesley only cared about one person and that was Wesley. So how could I trust the words coming out of his mouth? Before I even knew it, I agreed.

"Until then, we can meet secretly and you know that Chase will have his guys on me. It'll have to be once a week and we'll have to be out of town."

He looked at me, smiled, and said, "I know the perfect place."

"Okay, I will email the information. I know he will be tracking my phone," I smiled.

Wesley rubbed his temples, visibly aggravated.

"Just play the good wife while I get our ducks in a row," he told me.

I loved how he always took charge. That was why Chase and Carlton were threatened by him. I was more worried by Carlton than Chase. Chase was superficial, Carlton was a money-hungry savage.

"I need you to be careful around Carlton, babe," I whined.

Wesley flashed his million-dollar smile, then huffed, "I got this, babe, I know he's on some slick shit."

CARLTON

"Afon, we have to handle Wesley," I fumed.

Afon looked at me with his piercing green eyes.

"Why would I bite the hand that feeds us?" joked Afon.

I was pissed that he gave Wesley's ass so much credit, and never once me. Afon was a Russian nationalist who was also an interpreter for foreign businessmen. Ever since we were younger, I admired his fairness and how he always balanced his double life. He was intimidating to most—he stood six foot five, around two hundred sixty-five pounds with blonde hair and emerald eyes. He was a former military sniper, highly decorated. He was a quiet storm.

"Also, I'm hearing he has ties to the murder of Ortiz' son," I confirmed. "We don't need that type of heat from the Italians." Afon rubbed his chin, listening intently. "I mean we have too much to lose, boss."

Afon smiled, then said, "I remember a time when you all were younger and you would've taken a bullet for him without hesitation. What happened to those days?" smiled a reflective Afon as he swished his vodka.

"Boss, we're a multi-million-dollar operation now," I responded. "We're no longer the two ragged, unkempt black kids. We're men you groom to run this empire." I could tell Afon was disappointed by my response. His demeanor changed.

His voice dropped. "I corrupted you both with the finer things in life." I paced back and forth now. "Sit your ass down," commanded Afon. "I don't agree with killing Wesley, but if that's what you feel you have to do, then do it. I guess blood isn't thicker than water. Did you ever consider getting rid of the bitch?"

Afon's expression was one of disgust as he stood to leave with his three Russian goons in tow.   Damn, he was right. Maybe I should just kill the bitch.

***

I still needed Camille to tell me what the fuck she would do. I had that little smart-mouth bitch Yawnha, at a house with some bad friends and it was her move. I felt like my request was simple, but these bitches were stupid. If she kept playing games, I would make her watch me kill her family. I couldn't have her fucking up my money.

I sent her ass a text telling her that she had three days before her niece was a dead bitch.

WESLEY

As I pulled up to see Afon, I saw Carlton leaving and he seemed pissed. I could only imagine that he was plotting on my life. What did it matter in this lifestyle? It was kill or be killed. It was fucked up that I may have to kill my cousin who I thought was my brother from another mother. All because he wanted to fuck my bitch. I parked my car in front of him. He looked at me as I jumped out.

"What up?"

"I thought you'd be out chasing pussy."

"I was looking for Camille. Have you seen her?"

He looked at the ground before saying, "That cop killed her."

I was stunned. Why would Chase kill Camille? Damn, was Alexis safe? We stared at each other, not saying a word. Then I asked, "How do you know Chase killed Camille?"

He looked at me for a moment, shocked that I asked the question.

"He told me he did."

"You fraternizing with the enemy now, Carlton?"

All I could think was that my babe was right. Carlton and Chase were working together to take me down. Damn, I thought Carlton and I were better than that.

"Nah, nothing like that. I had to get the heat off us somehow. You won't stop fucking the nigga's bitch."

"I love Alexis, so it's more than just fucking his bitch. I had her first; she belongs to me. However, she made it clear that it was over; I was just some good dick and she's going to marry him in a couple of hours."

Carlton smiled at what he thought was my pain. I tried to give extra sad look to make him believe it was over between Alexis and me. I needed Carlton to trust me again. If we both lost, he'd be happy but if I got her, it would be death by Wesley.

"Well, you win some, you lose some. It's fucked up that you lost to the white boy. She got all that ass and it's going to be bunching on his white dick."

"Yeah, it's all good. Alexis deserves to be happy and I can't give her what she needs."

Carlton walked past me without replying to my comment. I could tell that he was pissed but I had to let it go. I walked into the house and I was greeted by my two favorite goons. They never took my weapons, but they escorted me into the meeting area. Afon sat at the table with a cup of tea. I joined him. He looked very intense as I sat down.

"Hello, Wes, for what do I owe this pleasure?"

"I'm sorry to stop my unannounced, but I need to speak with you."

"Speak."

"Carlton is working with a cop and I think they want to kill me. Yes, it is about Alexis, but I have always done my job, so I just want to know if this is on your request."

"Hell, no. I would never work with a pig and if I wanted you dead, you would be dead. You have to handle things the way you see fit. I won't get in the middle of this shit with you and Carlton. But I will say this—watch your back."

He didn't have to say any more. I knew then that Carlton was really out to get me, but why? *What the fuck did I do to him?*

I guess blood wasn't thicker than water.

ALEXIS

I waited about twenty minutes after Wesley left and then I got in my car and headed home. My mind was deep in thought about the conversation we just had. I honestly couldn't imagine that Carlton would be pissed off because he couldn't have me. There had to be something else going on between him and Wesley. Carlton had never even said hi to me; okay, maybe that's the only thing he ever said to me. He always gave me an evil eye, looking at me like he wanted to kill me. Hell, I figured he hated me.

The sound of my cell phone startled me and I almost jumped through the roof of my car. I looked down and saw it was Chase. He wondered where the heck I was, probably scared that I would stand him up. I answered the phone.

"Hey."

"Where the fuck are you?"

"I had to do some last-minute errands. I'll still meet you at the courthouse."

"Okay, just wanted to make sure I was good. Hadn't heard from you."

"Chase, can I ask you a question?"

"What's up, babe?"

"Why are you and Carlton so friendly? Tell me when did y'all become best friends? I thought he was Public Enemy Number Two."

"Can we not talk about Wesley or Carlton for once please, Alexis? Can't I just have one day?"

"No choice, we need to talk about it. I won't go down the aisle with you if I think you're plotting to kill Wesley. So, you have some explaining to do. I want to know why. I want to know what the plan is and you're going to tell me, or you can marry yourself. This is all childish games. If you wouldn't have been fucking Camille, we would've had our separation."

"Are you going to just keep throwing that in my face? Yes, I fucked Camille. I made a mistake, but you had sex with Wesley too. So what makes your sins better than mine?"

I wanted to just kill his manhood and tell him how his sex was whack and how I went back to Wesley because he knew how to give it to me like a real man. I decided against it. I really needed to know what the plan was so that I could keep Wesley safe.

I softened my tone before saying, "Chase, we're trying to make this work. I don't want any secrets between us, not anymore. I need you to be a hundred percent honest with me and tell me what's going on between you and Carlton. You can't trust him; he isn't who he appears to be."

"Do you honestly think I don't know how to judge people, Alexis? I know that he's a miserable sack of shit, but I'm already in too deep."

"Why would you get involved with him anyways?"

"Why are you asking me twenty questions like this? Alexis, we're about to get married. Let it go."

Chase had just pissed me off. Without another word, I ended the call and went to the house. Chase's car was there. A part of me hoped that his ass would be somewhere else. To my surprise, there was another car in the yard. Once out of the car, I quickly made my way to the door and heard voices.

"Man, we need to leave Wesley alone. He and Alexis are over."

"He told me that today. But I don't believe it. Plus, it will just be another bitch after her. He chases too many bitches; he has to go."

"Why would you want to kill your flesh and blood, Carlton?"

"He isn't focused on our money, and fucking with that will get you killed."

Abruptly, I opened the door to the house and Carlton glared at me. There was no need to say anything. I made my way to the bedroom, closing the door behind me. Moments later, it opened and there stood Carlton.

"Leave."

He took three steps closer to me, and grabbed me by the arm, twisting it a little.

"You just gonna marry this white boy and play my cousin. For real bitch, you could've fucked with me."

"Chase! Chase!" I screamed.

"He went to the car. I'm not going to hurt you, Alexis. We're just talking."

Thank God Chase forced me to take all of those self-defense classes; it helped me to get away from his crazy ass.

"Carlton, you slide straight to hell," I yelled as I kneed him right in the groin, running out the bedroom and right into Chase.

"Babe, are you okay?"

Before responding to his stupid ass, I smacked the shit out of him. "You brought that crazy bastard into our life and you better get him out. Do you understand?"

Carlton lay on the floor in our bedroom, moaning in pain. Chase just looked at me with a smirk, pissing me off. If we weren't about to be in the spotlight, he would've had a black eye. After Carlton was off the floor, I threw on my wedding dress and we left. Imagine my surprise to see Carlton at the reception hall.

Waltzing over to Chase who looked very perplexed, I whispered in his ear, "Why is your boyfriend here?"

"I was wondering the same thing," he replied.

Chase went to speak with Carlton, who was tossing back drinks. I went to a quiet area so that I could call Wesley.

He didn't answer and it made me mad. How could a married woman be upset that her other man hadn't answered the phone when she called? I was about to be in Rome for two weeks; hopefully, I could see him before we left.

WESLEY

Damn was the only thing I could think as I watched the love of my life marrying another man. Yes, I showed up at the courthouse, peeping in like a lost puppy. Hell, a nigga even shed a few tears. My Alexis didn't even look happy. Yes, she was beautiful as ever, but she was miserable. After the wedding, I needed a fucking drink. Ten shots later, I was at my crib passed out. I woke up at two a.m. to Alexis throwing ice-cold water on me. As much as I wanted to be upset, I couldn't. It was a pleasure just seeing her chocolate ass.

"Damn, baby, what the fuck is wrong with you?"

"Do you know that I have been calling your ass for hours? You fucking had me worried sick about you."

She was cussing my ass out, looking sexy as fuck in short black lingerie with matching heels. I grabbed her up and kissed her. She wrapped her arms around me, breaking the kiss and putting her head on my chest. I squeezed her, feeling her tears on my shirt.

"Baby, I'm sorry. I didn't mean to worry you. I was just sad that you had married Chase so I got drunk."

"You can't just get drunk and pass out, babe. Your cousin is trying to kill you. He wants Chase to help him. He was at the house, then he was at the wedding and the reception. He is trying to catch us lying. He snatched me up yesterday."

"He did what?"

"Yes, babe, twisted my arm behind my back, only hurting enough to get my attention. Told me that I should've gotten with him. You can't handle him right now. If you do, he will know that we were together."

She made a great point, but I wanted to put a bullet in his head. Every dog had his day and Carlton's day was coming soon.

"How much time do you have?" I questioned her.

"Chase got called into work. He has to finish some things before we leave for Rome next week."

"How long are y'all going to be in Rome?"

"Two weeks?"

"That's too fucking long. Alexis, what the fuck am I supposed to do for two weeks without my chocolate drop?"

"Come up with a plan to get rid of Carlton. I think we can use me as bait."

I shot her a dirty look and kissed her—my way of changing the subject. We kissed awhile, staring into each other's eyes and for a moment, I just wanted to run away with her. Just wanted to keep her to myself and not send her back to Chase. She straddled me, which was perfect. I got to make love to the bride and I planned on putting in extra work. She wouldn't be making love to her husband tonight.

Suddenly, she jumped up and made a mad dash to the restroom. I heard her throwing up.

"Babe, are you okay?"

"Yeah, I must have food poisoning."

Seven minutes later, she was back, standing in front of me, naked. Her breasts stared at me, her nipples hard. She was the perfect painting; a part of me wanted to admire her beauty and the other part needed to be inside her.

"Are you just going to look at me?"

Alexis made her way to the bed. She attempted to straddle me, but I wanted to taste her sweet juices. As soon as she was on the bed, I went out for dinner. I ate her pussy, making her cum back to back to back. She begged me to stop and I did for five seconds, telling her that she shouldn't taste so good. An hour later, I finally entered her, giving her slow strokes. She was wet. Don't get me wrong, she was always wet, but tonight there was something different about her and the way she reacted to my touch. We spent the rest of the time enjoying each other.

Damn, I loved the hell out of this woman.

ALEXIS

I was so sure that Wesley was back to his old tricks. I expected to find his ass booed up with some bitch. I was ready to cut his ass and he was just passed out. Finally, he was making the effort that I was, and I was so happy. For the first time, I felt like he loved me and he made love to me all night and all morning. It was fucked up that I spent my wedding night making love to another man. But shit happens.

I woke to breakfast in bed followed by a kiss on the cheek. "Who in the hell was this man and what the fuck did he do with Wes?" I teased, smiling from ear to ear. I took a sip of the orange juice and had to run to the bathroom and throw up. This was the second time this happened. What the fuck was going on with me? I got back in the bed.

"Babe, you okay?"

"Yes, I must be getting some stomach bug."

"I have some runs to make. For the record, I want to see you as much as possible before you leave. Make that happen."

Shaking my head to let him know that was doable, my focus was on the last time I had a cycle.

Damn, I think I'm pregnant. As soon as Wes left, I jumped my ass out of bed and went to the drugstore, grabbing a few home pregnancy tests. When I got back to the apartment, I was happy to find Chase not home and it appeared that he hadn't been there all night.

First thing first, a hot bath called my name. My private area needed a soak because a bitch was sore as fuck from Wesley. Why did his dick have to be so fucking big? While in the tub, I attempted to come up with a plan.

It had been about eight months and for the last five, Wesley and I had been having sex and not using protection. So, if these tests come back positive, things just got complicated.

Once my bath was over, I peed on the stick and all seven tests came back positive. *Damn, what the fuck am I supposed to do now?*

Shit just can't be easy for Alexis. A part of me always wanted to carry Wes' baby, but this shit looked super bad. Married to one, pregnant by the next.

Damn was the only thought pressing my head. Should I at least tell Wesley? After composing myself, I finally got ready for work and while I was on the way there, I stopped back at the drugstore to get some stuff for my upset stomach.

To my surprise, there was Camille. I had no intention on talking to her, but she approached me.

"Hey, can we chat?"

"Why?"

"I need to get the hell away from here and I think that you are the person to help me."

"You fucked my man. Both of you tried to ruin my relationship with Chase and you want me to help you?"

"Look, Alexis, I'm sorry but I did what I was told to do."

"Now I'm telling you to get out of my face."

I walked away from her. The nerve of this bitch to ask me for help after she tried to destroy me. She was lucky that I didn't let the hood come out and beat her ass in this store. By the time I made it to work, Chase was blowing up my phone.

"Yes, Chase." I answered.

"Where are you?"

"Work."

"Sorry, I didn't make it home last night. I fell asleep working on this missing teen story. I may need your help."

"With what?"

"A sixteen-year-old was taken from her school a few days ago, and I may need some media coverage. A school full of people and no one saw anything. One thing, though. This is Camille's niece."

"Are you still fucking that bitch? When is y'alls baby due, Chase?"

"Alexis, I'm the fucking police. I have to help people."

"Fuck you, Chase." I said, hanging up on him.

He called back, but I decided to turn my phone off. He had me fucked up if he thought I would help his bitch out.

CAMILLE

My phone went off and I got a picture of what appeared to be my niece Yawnha. Immediately, I called her and her phone went to voicemail and my heart raced. I called my sister and she said that Yawnha was at school and it was normal for her not to answer.

Since the message came from Carlton, I decided I better call him. After one hundred times, he didn't answer. All he did was send a picture of my niece, tied and beaten. *Who the fuck does that to a kid? What type of monster is he?* I really didn't want to get an abortion. But I would do whatever it took to get my niece back.

I replied to the message, telling him that he won. I would get rid of my baby. Even though that wasn't the plan at all. I had a friend who was pregnant and I could change the paperwork so that he thought that I got the abortion. Then I would leave for a few months, have my baby, then make all their asses pay for crossing me.

That was on Friday and it was now a week later on Friday again and I still hadn't heard from Carlton. I hated having to watch my family go crazy because our baby was missing. I got in touch with Chase and I asked him to help me, but I knew that he was working with Carlton. He acted concerned, like he didn't know. I showed him the proof that I had an abortion and he was happy. So happy that he let me give his ass head but I recorded it this time. As soon as I finished, he told me that he married Alexis. That meant Wesley was lonely.

Maybe he and I could come together and he could stop talking about being with Alexis. I called him but it went straight to voicemail. I had a huge headache so I walked in the store and there was Alexis. I thought she was pretty and after that threesome the other day, I craved pussy. I never imagined that I would want to be with a woman but lately all I think about was tasting some pussy. From what I heard, she must have good pussy; all these men tried to get a taste.

I smiled at her, but she wasn't feeling me at all. I decided to say hi and ask for her help. It didn't go the way I planned. She was pissed that I fucked Chase and Wesley. I should've told her that I was still sucking Chase's dick. Soon enough she would find out.

If something happened to my Yawnha, all hell would break loose.

CHASE

Finally marrying the woman of my dreams and I spent my wedding night getting head from some stripper. Why in the hell couldn't I shake this addiction to Camille? Her head was fire, that's why. When Alexis and I got to Rome, I would tell her that she needed to better her head game. After that, I would be good. It was the only thing missing. Oh well, for the last few months, we hadn't had much sex. Tonight, she would have to give me some ass. But hell, we couldn't get along.

Damn, did we marry for the right reason? No matter what, I would make my marriage work. Wesley didn't get the prize. I loved Alexis and we looked good together, but were looks everything?

It was fucked up for me to ask Alexis to help Camille. That was stupid as hell. In the last five months, I had fallen in love with a stripper and gotten involved with drug dealers. Hell, I was one step away from being a bad officer. I guess I had better get this money. I had been intercepting drug deals so that the supplier wouldn't trust Wesley anymore. What Carlton failed to realize was that it looked bad on his ass as well; they were a team and if one part fell short, the whole fucking team was fucked up for real.

***

I had to work with Carlton for two fucking hours. All I wanted to do was get home to my wife who was pissed with me. She said that she would be hanging with Michael. I wanted to have a romantic evening, but looked like we had to save that for Rome. Thank God, we were leaving tomorrow. I got home and Alexis was nowhere to be found. *Damn, where the fuck is she?* I got in the shower, went into the bedroom, noticing that our bags weren't packed.

In an effort to keep things running smooth, I packed up our clothes. Alexis had bought a new wardrobe for the trip so it was easy. Just as I was about to call Alexis, the front door opened. She walked in looking beautiful. She wore a form-fitting strapless black dress, some silver earrings, a matching silver purse, and matching shoes. She smiled at me and headed to the bathroom. Without a word, I followed her. As soon as she turned around to see me, I grabbed her, kissing her passionately and trying to undress her.

"Not tonight, Chase. I need to pack our stuff and it has been a long day."

"Babe, we just got married and I want to make love to my wife. Is that too much to ask?" I yelled.

She dropped the dress to the floor, exposing her naked body. She grabbed me by the hand, forcing me to the bed.

Once naked, she rode me, doing all types of things that she had never done before, forcing me to release in ten minutes flat. Alexis got off me and made her way to the bathroom to shower.

Thirty minutes later, Alexis was back in the room. She smiled when she noticed that I had packed the bags for us.

"Well, Mr. Manchester, you packed our bags?"

"Yes, I did, Mrs. Manchester. It was the helpful thing to do."

Alexis moved in to kiss me when my work phone rang. That was just Carlton, I thought. A part of me wanted to answer, but I was tired of being his bitch. After my honeymoon, I would have my boys raid his place. This was becoming a hassle.

WESLEY

Alexis came through and spent the day with me. Before she had left, she hit me with some big news. Her ass was pregnant and was almost one hundred percent sure that it was mine. We planned to get a blood test as soon as she got back in town.

For sure, it was time for me to stop hitting the streets. I hated that she even married that whack-ass cop now. She should be here with me. I wondered if she told him that she was pregnant. I was pissed, not to mention his ass was still fucking with me and my crew.

Carlton had to be telling him where the drop off was. He raided left and right Elle and Afon were pissed and I had to come up with a solution. Therefore, tonight I gave Carlton a different location than I did Elle. I told Afon that Carlton was trying to ruin me and he simply said handle it. If I did, I could get myself clean. I wouldn't get out but I would be sitting next to him.

Back to my snake-ass cousin. As soon as I gave his ass an address, I watched him make calls and send text messages. While at the bar, I had one of the strippers give him a drink laced with sleep aids. I had to have her get me his phone.

Let's pray that tonight's drink mixture wouldn't kill his snake ass. I just wanted to make sure that he was out cold, so I added four pills in some Crown, making sure the pills dissolved.

After his drink was served, Camille greeted me.

"Give me my fucking niece back?" she demanded.

"What the fuck are you talking about?"

She ranted on about how we kidnapped her and she showed me messages from Carlton. I fucking threw up in my mouth. Why the fuck would he do that?

"Look, Camille, I don't fuck with kids, not at all. I would've just shot ya ass in the stomach. Problem solved, no baby. Get the fuck out of my face and get Carlton."

She stared at me for a few moments and then walked away.

Carlton had to be stopped.

***

As soon as Alexis got back, she was at my apartment. I came home to her, sitting on the counter. It was a lovely surprise. After us hugging and kissing, I wanted to jump all over her, but we needed to talk about our plan. First, I didn't want to risk her being seen coming in and out of my place. While she was gone, I rented a hotel an hour out of town. I told her that we could meet there weekly, squeezing in time around here. I had a plan to keep Chase on bogus-ass runs. I called Carlton, telling him that I was at a run, giving him an address. There would be a small rival gang there just to make it look as if the feds were cracking down on crime in general, and that would help to mend things with Elle.

I filled Alexis in on how Chase had been helping Carlton try to ruin me and how they were talking every day. I also told her that I thought that Carlton had done something to Camille's niece. I had been searching for her, but I couldn't find her. I still had time to find her, but it broke my heart. It had been a month, but I also hadn't heard from Camille since the day she told me. I had given Afon and Elle all the proof I had about Chase and Carlton working together. Man, he couldn't work that close with a cop in the world. He had better hope that he didn't end up dead first.

"Babe, we have to fake my death for us to get out. You need to be first on the scene and I have the prefect victim."

"Okay, babe, that is a great idea."

We kissed and soon I was making love to her again. I texted Carlton five addresses that would keep Chase busy with paperwork while I made love to his wife.

Back to the Present

CARLTON

My phone had been blowing up for hours. Finally, I noticed that it was Chase and I wanted to know why the fuck he was calling me.

"What?" I yelled into the phone.

"Wesley is dead." Chase blurted out.

My soul jumped for joy. After being pissed that I didn't get to kill his ass myself. Things all worked out. For a moment, I thought that he had figured out I was after him, but I was smarter.

"Again, why are you on my phone?"

"You are next of kin and will need to claim the body. He was set on fire so it was a crime of passion. It will be on the news soon. We can't release a name yet. I just saw Alexis pull up."

"Tell her it is for the best. His ass needed to die."

"Carlton, now that Wesley is gone, our business is done."

"You are done when I say and we aren't done. I need a partner."

He hung up on me and texted me an address. I got dressed and headed there. I hit up Afon and broke the bad news to him.

When I got there, some guy said that there was hair and an ID. That's how they knew that it was Wesley. My day had just gotten better and Chase was about to take Wesley's spot, if he knew what was good for Alexis. Just as the thought left my head, Chase stood in front of me.

"Just the man I wanted to see." I said.

"What?"

"We need to take over the streets since Wesley is gone."

"We ain't doing shit."

"If you want to be with your wife, you will help me. The only person keeping her alive is YOU."

We glared at each other and this was a crock of shit. He walked away looking pissed. I would never let him forget that he was a cop. He helped me so far now he was in too deep. Damn, I needed to get in touch with Camille. I returned her niece home; she was broken but would like to see another day. After I sent her home, I hadn't seen or heard from Camille. She quit dancing and went MIA.

ALEXIS

So far, our plan was going perfect. I had to chat with Chase. He had to break the news to me. I saw him talking with a few of his men until he saw me. He came over, placed his arms around my neck, and told me it was Wesley.

Now it was time for me to give the performance of the year. I screamed and fell to the ground, crying like I had just lost my best friend. I wish I could've patted myself on the back a few times. Chase tried to comfort me, but he knew that I loved Wes all my life and that this would be hard for me.

I wouldn't see Wesley for a few days. Then he would call me and let me know what to do next. I was worried he wouldn't want to go a few days without calling; I got a burner phone so we should be cool. I just had to figure out how the hell I would get away from Chase. It had been two months since I found out that I was pregnant. Now it was time to tell my husband, but after I went live for breaking news.

After giving another Oscar-winning performance, I made my way back to work. I requested some time off and my manager had a great idea. I should take a case that was out of town so I could get a break. I declined because I needed the time off, but then again, it was a perfect cover story when I heard from Wesley. We had to make sure that our plan would work, and then we would meet up. As soon as he called, I would be out of town with an assignment that would get me a few months off away.

***

It had been three weeks and there was no word from Wesley. I guess he just used me to get away from all the madness and he would leave me a single parent. I had to tell Chase that I was pregnant. I was starting to show.

I was walking from my job to the car when I felt someone grab me from behind. I could feel a gun or what I thought was a gun in my back.

"Scream, Alexis, and I will blow your brains out."

That was the one and only Carlton. It was easier to just comply with his orders versus trying to see if he would really shoot me.

There was no need for small talk. He was talking to me for a reason; I just had no idea what he wanted. Since there was no Wesley, he really would leave me alone.

Then it dawned on me. Whatever he wanted with me had to do with Chase. Damn, what type of mess did he get me into?

To my surprise, he only took me to the club. He told me that I needed to call Chase and tell him that I had six hours to live if he didn't comply. As soon as Chase answered the phone, I told him that I was pregnant and I had been kidnapped because he was working with the enemy and now I would die.

Carlton didn't give us much time to chat. After I said my peace, he locked me in a room, saying that he would be back. He had to teach Chase a lesson; he just wanted to fuck me.

"You don't have to rape me. I will just have sex with you," I pleaded.

He didn't force himself on me, but he did have sex with me and recorded it. I cried the whole time as he had a gun next to my head. It had to be hours later, I was lying in a bed feeling like the dirtiest person in the world. Finally, the burner phone rang.

"Alexis, I got us a place."

Those were the best words I had heard, but how in the hell did I get out of here?

"Carlton has me. I can't meet you. I have no clue how to get out."

"Where are you?"

"At the club, in the bedroom."

"Behind the bookcase is a door. It leads you to the basement. Inside the wine cellar, go to the right and there is a door. Find Chris and he will take you to the bus station. You leave with the shirt on your back and call this number. I will tell you where to go."

The line went dead and I made my way to the cellar. And all the way to the bus station, I called the number back and there was no answer. I went on the first bus out. I guess Alexis was on her own.

TO BE CONTUINED………

Check out other reads by Black Beauty Presents

Every Bit of Crazy by Deidre Leshay

Quiet Storm by Deidre Leshay

This Type of Love Features Deidre Leshay

Baddies Only 1 &2 Vixen

Verses & Lyrics Vixen

Christmas Isn't Always Merry Feat R. Coxton

Thug Angel by Jeff Carroll

Gold Digger Killer by Jeff Carroll

From the Prison to the Palace LaShawn

CPSIA information can be obtained
at www.ICGtesting.com
Printed in the USA
LVOW10s1614130318
569703LV00016B/932/P